'I can't read you. I never quite know what you're going to do next. Fascinating.' The curve of his lips made it clear that was a compliment.

She knew it was just Leo's charm—his way of turning a situation around and removing the barbs. But it was still compelling, and when she looked into his eyes she felt that he really did find her fascinating.

Alex swallowed hard. 'You know what, Leo? Even if you could read minds you still wouldn't be able to see into the future.'

'I think the universe has something to answer for there. We can see the past, but it's too late to go back and do things differently. And the future…' He shrugged.

The one timeframe that mattered most was the one that Leo seemed unable to get to grips with.

'What

Dear Reader,

Science fiction has taught us that using time travel to meddle with the past isn't always the wisest course of action. One small thing changes and it sets off a cascade of alternative realities, any one of which might have unintended consequences.

When Alex and Leo first meet they're dressed up as space travellers from their favourite TV show. That meeting sets a chain of events in place which reverberates through their lives, and when they meet again the night that they shared together all those years ago has become an irrevocable part of who they have both become.

It's an often-posed question. What would you do differently? But, although it's always good to learn from the past, it's not something that any of us can change. The present might be fleeting, and the future unknown, but that allows us the great gift of hope. One of the things I most enjoyed about writing Leo and Alex's story was seeing Leo gradually turn away from his past and learn to hope for a better future.

I hope that you enjoy Alex and Leo's story. I'm always thrilled to hear from readers, and you can contact me via my website: annieclaydon.com.

Annie x

THE DOCTOR'S DIAMOND PROPOSAL

BY
ANNIE CLAYDON

Published in Great Britain 2016
By Mills & Boon, an imprint of HarperCollins*Publishers*
1 London Bridge Street, London, SE1 9GF

© 2016 Annie Claydon

ISBN: 978-0-263-92626-2

Printed and bound in Spain
by CPI, Barcelona

Cursed with a poor sense of direction and a propensity to read, **Annie Claydon** spent much of her childhood lost in books. A degree in English Literature followed by a career in computing didn't lead directly to her perfect job—writing romance for Mills & Boon—but she has no regrets in taking the scenic route. She lives in London: a city where getting lost can be a joy.

Visit the Author Profile page at
millsandboon.co.uk for more titles.

To my wonderful editor, Nicola Caws.
With grateful thanks for your guiding hand on this journey.

Praise for
Annie Claydon

CHAPTER ONE

Ten years ago...

THE PARTY HAD got off to a slow start, but by eleven o'clock the house was packed with people and Leo Cross was beginning to feel hot and uncomfortable in his costume.

It had seemed like a good idea at the time. *Orion Shift* was less of a TV show to the six medical students who shared the sprawling house in West London and more of a Friday evening ritual. The one hour in the week that didn't belong to study, girlfriends or the urgent need for sleep. So what better way to celebrate their third year exam results than decorate the living room with as much tinfoil as they could get their hands on and suspend inflatable planets from the ceiling?

Dressing up as the crew of the interstellar spacecraft *Orion Shift* had been the next logical step. But a hot summer's evening wasn't really the time to be wearing a heavy jacket with a high collar, and Leo was beginning to wish that personal temperature regulation fields really had been invented.

A girl in blue body paint and a leotard sidled up to him. 'Captain Boone! You look particularly delicious tonight.'

'Maddie. How are you doing?'

'You want a Tellurian cocktail?' Maddie draped her arms around Leo's shoulders. Clearly she and Pete had been arguing again. It was only a matter of time before the inevitable reconciliation, but at the moment Pete was on the other side of the room taking a great deal of interest in a red-haired girl dressed as a Fractalian hydra and Maddie had clearly decided that she was going to give him a taste of his own medicine.

Leo disentangled himself from Maddie's grip. 'No. Thanks, but…' *Just no*. If Pete and Maddie wanted to play games that was fine, but Leo knew better than to get involved.

'Leo…!' Maddie stuck out her lower lip in a disappointed pout as he retreated quickly through the press of people.

He pushed his way to the kitchen, avoiding the usual group around the beer keg, and slipped outside into the back garden, sighing with relief as the warm breeze brushed his face. The paved space at the back of the house was packed with people, drinking and talking, and Leo made good his escape, dodging across the grass and into the pool of darkness that lay beneath the trees at the end of the garden.

He bumped into something soft and sweet-smelling and saw a flash of silvery-green luminescence. A shadow detached itself from the other shadows and stumbled into a pool of moonlight. It was Lieutenant Tara Xhu to a T.

'Another fugitive?' A smile played around her lips.

'You could say that. So how did you manage to make it out of there?'

Tara—or whatever her real name was—shrugged. 'I'm not sure. I've only watched one episode, and that was to get the costume right, so I don't really know what Tara's strategy might be.' Her mouth twitched suddenly into a flirtatious smile. 'So you're Captain Boone?'

Leo's eyes were beginning to adjust to the darkness and the more they did so, the more he liked what he saw. She was dressed all in black, thick leggings, boots and an off the shoulder top that followed her slim curves and displayed the green scales which spread across Tara's shoulder. A fair replica of an immobility gun was strapped to her thigh and twisted metallic strands ran round her fingers and across the back of her hands. Her dark hair was streaked with green and anchored in a spiky arrangement on the top of her head with Tara's silver dagger pins.

Leo had been in love at first sight before, but suddenly the other times didn't seem anything like the real thing. She raised one jewelled eyebrow and Leo realised that his gaze had been following the path of the scales that ran down the side of her face and neck and disappeared beneath her top.

'Um… Great costume. Your scales look…really lifelike.' Captain Thomas Boone would undoubtedly have managed something a bit more urbane, but then he had more experience of the galaxy than Leo.

'Thanks. Iridescent body paint. I felt a bit of an idiot on the bus, on my way here.' She grinned at him and moved back towards the old picnic bench which stood under the trees. 'So are you really escaping something, or do you just want some fresh air?'

'A bit of both.' Leo sat down next to her, stretching his legs out in front of him. This replica Tara had a lightness about her movements, a kind of joy about her, which broke through the warlike quality of the real Tara's appearance. Even though she was sitting a good two feet away from him, Leo could almost feel her warmth.

'You live here?'

'Yes.'

'Then you must be a medical student.'

'That's right. Starting year four in a couple of weeks, so this'll probably be the last party we have for a while.'

'I hear it's a tough year. An interesting one, though…'

That was exactly how Leo felt about it. He knew that his clinical attachment was going to be hard work, but he couldn't wait to start putting all that he'd learned into practice. 'What do you do?'

She shrugged. 'Nothing at the moment. I'm just back from a year in Australia.'

'Yeah? What's it like?' All Leo wanted to do right now was sit here in the darkness and listen to her talk.

She laughed. 'Bit too big to describe in one sentence. I loved it, though.'

Leo imagined that she'd taken every moment of the last year and squeezed the very most out of it, in the same way that she seemed to be draining every drop of potential from these moments. It was infectious.

She was fiddling thoughtfully with the bright silver strands across the back of her hand. 'Did you always want to do medicine?'

'Yeah. My uncle's a doctor, and when I was nine I saw him save someone's life. That settled it for me, and there's never been anything else I wanted to do.'

She nodded quietly. 'So you have a calling. A mission in life.'

Sometimes, poring over his books late at night, it didn't seem so. But Tara made it all sound like something special.

'Yeah. Guess I do.'

'I'm still looking for mine. There are so many possibilities and I don't think I can settle on just one. So I'm going to be helping out on my dad's farm for the next year while I think about putting in my university applications.'

'You'll find the right thing.' Leo applied all of the weight of his twenty-one years to the problem. And all of the certainty from the last five minutes, that whatever she decided to do she'd do it wholeheartedly.

'I suppose I will.' She seemed to ponder the idea for a moment, then smiled suddenly. 'Nothing like mucking out to concentrate the mind on your aspirations for the future.'

'Would you like me to go and get you a drink?' Leo hoped she'd say yes. That they could continue this conversation alone, out here, rather than going back to the heat and noise of the party.

'Thanks, but no. I tried one of those blue cocktails and it was too sweet.' She hesitated, then seemed to come to a decision. 'That coffee bar around the corner. Think it'll still be open?'

'It's open all night.' Sweet promise stirred in Leo's chest.

'You fancy making a break for it, then?'

Theirs weren't the most outlandish costumes amongst the coffee bar's customers that night, but she had still tugged awkwardly at her green hair and silver jewellery. Leo had laughingly persuaded her to stay just as she was, saying that since he was dressed as a spaceship captain, it was practically expected that his First Lieutenant should be accompanying him.

They'd talked all night, fuelled by coffee and then ham and cheese toasties at three in the morning. At six, she'd refused to allow him to see her all the way home and he'd had to content himself with walking her to the bus stop.

'May I call you?' Leo made a silent wish that the bus wouldn't come just yet.

'I was hoping you would.' She smiled at him, reaching into her jacket for her phone and reeling off the number. Leo repeated it over in his head, his fingers shaking unaccountably as he pressed the keys. He hit dial, and her phone chimed. Even her ringtone seemed fresh and full of joy.

'That's it.' She rejected the call and gratifyingly saved his number.

'Lieutenant Tara.' Leo grinned, spelling out the words as he typed them into his phone. 'What's your real name, though?'

'Alex...' She turned as a bus drew up at the stop. 'This one's mine. You will call, won't you...?'

'Yes.' Leo wondered whether it would be appropriate to kiss her goodbye and decided that he'd already missed his chance. The night had been perfect as it stood, a meeting of minds that had nothing to do with any alien powers, and when he kissed her he wanted enough time to do it properly. She got onto the bus, pressing her ticket against the reader, and turned to wave at him.

The bus drew away. Calling her now would be too soon. He turned to walk back home, and his phone buzzed.

May we meet in other worlds.

Her text mimicked Tara's habitual farewell.

And get some sleep.

Leo grinned, texting back his reply, watching until the bus turned a corner and disappeared.

He called that evening and she didn't reply. Perhaps she'd decided to have an early night. The next day she didn't reply either.

Leo counted the number of calls he made, knowing that each one would show up on her phone. Half a dozen was beginning to look a little stalkerish, so he sent a text instead.

No answer. He left it a week and called again, leaving a carefully scripted voicemail and resolving that if she didn't reply this time he'd take the hint and give up. Clearly, the gorgeous, vivacious Lieutenant Tara had decided that, of all the glittering possibilities she saw ahead of her, he wasn't one of them. It was time to retreat gracefully and get on with the next chapter of his life.

CHAPTER TWO

Time warp to the present day...

ALEXANDRA JACKSON WAS shaking as she walked across the large marble-clad reception area of the hotel. The receptionist gave her directions to the coffee lounge.

'Oh, and where's the ladies' room, please?' She still had ten minutes to spare, and her heart was beating like a hammer in her chest. She needed to calm down.

'Through there...'

Alex followed the receptionist's pointing finger, ending up in a tastefully decorated ante-room that was larger, and rather smarter, than her own lounge. Sitting down, she closed her eyes, concentrating on deep, slow breaths.

Leo Cross. She'd thought about him a lot in the last ten years, certainly more than one night in a coffee bar would warrant. Maybe because of what had happened on her way home. The car that had swerved across the road and hit her, after she'd got off the bus, had changed everything.

Alex had wondered whether, by some chance, he might be one of the unending stream of doctors who stopped by her hospital bed, but he never had. She'd lost her phone and when her parents brought her a new one the number was different. In any case, what would he want with her now?

All the same, the memories of Leo's slightly awkward charm, the shining passion with which he'd talked about his ambition to become a doctor, had still lingered. Like a touchstone that stayed with her through the long months of convalescence, learning to walk again with a prosthetic leg, leaving home for university… Leo's commitment, his absolute certainty that he had a calling in life, had spurred her on. If he could do it, then so could she.

She'd hung onto the dream as long as she could, imagining Leo as some kind of white knight, a public health crusader—a starship captain, even. Nothing less would have been enough for Leo. But then she'd been brought back to earth with a bump.

Seven years after the night she'd met him, she saw Leo's name in the papers. Not believing it could be him, she'd searched the Internet for a picture. And there he was. The newest TV doctor, charming and urbane, who made an appearance at all the right parties. It seemed that the Leo she'd met had lost his ambition to change the world, and cashed in on his melting blue eyes and blond, handsome looks.

She'd thought about contacting him, but what would she say? That she'd held him in her heart for all these years until he became an ideal, rather than a blood and bone man? Perfect was best left where reality couldn't tarnish it, in dreams and the imagination.

But now Leo Cross had something she wanted.

Alex zipped up her bag and stood, straightening her jacket and smoothing her trousers. He wouldn't recognise her, nor would he remember. She could start again and pretend he was a completely different person from the one she'd met all those years ago.

As she walked into the coffee lounge she saw him immediately, sitting in one of the easy chairs grouped around each table. He still took her breath away. His hair was shorter and neater but still gave his face an almost angelic quality, even though the softness around his eyes had gone. He was dressed impeccably, a dark suit with an impossibly crisp white shirt and a subtly patterned, expensive-looking tie.

Everything about him screamed celebrity: the winter tan, the way the waiter knew exactly who he was and where he was sitting when Alex said who she was there to meet. She wondered whether the air of gravitas, lent by the pile of papers on his knee that were currently taking his full attention, was for her benefit and dismissed the thought. She was the one who needed to impress him, not the other way around.

He looked up as she approached, the sudden flash of uncertainty in his eyes giving way to recognition. Then he sprang to his feet, his papers dropping unheeded onto the carpet.

'Lieutenant Tara!' His smile was just as melting as it had ever been and the shock of being recognised and suddenly catapulted backwards in time left Alex momentarily at a loss. 'As I live and breathe… How are you? What have you been up to?'

'I think you know already. That's my PR bundle you've just dropped on the floor.'

He put two and two together with creditable speed. '*You're* Alexandra Jackson?'

'Yes. Only I prefer Alex…'

'Fewer syllables to contend with?' Leo's quiet, understated humour had remained intact, at least. She grinned up at him stupidly, a mixture of pleasure and panic rendering her silent.

'Did you know it was me?'

It was somehow engaging that he could even entertain the notion that someone could forget his smile. 'Yes. I didn't think you'd remember me.'

'Well, it's good to see you. I'm afraid I haven't had a chance to go through all the material you sent yet.' He bent to pick up the papers, shuffling the disorderly pile and laying it on the table.

She'd read every word of his PR material. Top of his class at medical school, and now practising as a GP in central London. An advanced diploma in counselling, and membership of a long list of professional bodies. Co-hosting a radio phone-in had quickly led to his own show, which aired three evenings a week, and then TV appearances, a couple of bestselling books and patronage of various health initiatives. On its own that was impressive, but if his social life was even half as interesting as the papers would have everyone believe, it was practically superhuman.

'So...' He gestured her towards the armchair standing opposite his. 'Shall we get down to business?'

'Yes. That would be good.' That was what she was here for. Not to spend the time gawping at Leo's smile.

'Right, then.' He seemed impatient now to start and Alex dumped her coat and bag onto an empty chair, sitting down quickly. 'I'd like to be honest with you about why you're here.'

That would be good. Alex nodded dumbly.

'Only I need your confirmation that this information will stay confidential. It'll be public knowledge soon, but I'd prefer it didn't come from anyone connected with us.'

'I understand. I won't say a word.'

'Thank you.' His stern look promised all kinds of retribution if she did. 'As you know 2KZ, the radio station I work for, holds an annual charity spotlight during February. And your charity applied to participate in that.'

'Yes. We were told before Christmas that our application wasn't successful.'

'It wasn't.' He paused to let that particular defeat sink in. 'But the charity we chose has had difficulties. We stuck by them for as long as the allegations were unsubstantiated but, now that they are, we have little choice but to look elsewhere.'

'And we have another chance?' Alex wondered which charity it was, and what the allegations were, but Leo's measured professionalism made it clear that he wasn't about to divulge that information.

'We considered abandoning our plans for this year completely, but we feel that a new charity, which we can investigate thoroughly for any sign of irregularity, would be an appropriate fallback position. The format would be slightly different—we'll be doing informal phone-ins instead of a series of pre-recorded programmes, because of the time factor. Are you still interested?'

Alex swallowed. 'This is a big project for us and it'll take a good proportion of our resources if we get involved. Can you tell me how far down the list we were?' Her feelings about being told that they were second best were irrelevant, even if Leo could have put it a little more tactfully. But she did need to know that 2KZ were interested enough to present her charity properly, and that they weren't just filling a few spare hours in their programming schedule.

'No. That would be inappropriate. But I can assure you that we're fully committed to going ahead with this and that I believe you're a good fit for the project. And I do need your answer now.'

In other words, she had to trust him. The old Leo would have been a lot easier to trust than this new one. But Alex knew she'd have to be crazy to pass up a chance like this.

'Yes, we're interested. Thank you. This is a wonderful opportunity for us.'

He dismissed her gratitude with a practised smile, a flip of his finger bringing a waiter over. 'Shall we have some tea? The Darjeeling, I think…' The waiter began to scribble on his pad.

She'd never been here before and had no idea what to order. All the same, Leo had left her to choose for herself at the coffee bar. Alex supposed that it had been a bit more straightforward then—coffee or tea, with or without milk. But it seemed that everything had been a bit more straightforward that night.

'That sounds nice. But I'd prefer Lady Grey if they have it.'

The ghost of a smile flickered around his lips. 'Lady Grey it is.' He looked up at the waiter. 'A pot for two, please.'

'Sandwiches or cakes, sir?' The waiter's gaze turned to Alex as Leo deflected the question her way.

'No, thank you. Not for me.' Dealing with Leo was taking all of her concentration. She wasn't sure she could manage cake crumbs as well.

Leo was shuffling through the papers in front of him on the table. 'Right. So your charity is called Together Our Way?'

'Yes.'

'No acronyms? Something a bit more snappy?'

'No.' Defiance bloomed suddenly in her chest. If they were going to do this, she was going to have to learn to stand up to Leo's steamroller tactics. 'We like to be referred to by our full name because it's the way we do things.'

'Yeah, I got that. And you're...' He caught a sheet from the pile which Alex recognised as her own CV. 'A qualified physiotherapist, and you founded Together Our Way to help young people with disabilities participate in sport.'

'Yes. I've brought some photographs with me that I think best show...'

'Later, maybe. I'd like to ask a bit about how the charity's run first.' He didn't even look at the pile of photos that Alex had pulled from her bag. 'From what I can see here, you're managing on a shoestring. You work three days a week as a physiotherapist and you don't take a salary from the charity. And you just have one part-time paid employee, who called me back yesterday to arrange this meeting. From what Rhona says, she seems to be doing rather more than I'd normally expect from a part-timer.'

'When people give us money, they want to see it spent on our core aims, not our running costs. We have an arrangement with Rhona that suits us both—she has family commitments and we give her very flexible working hours, and in return she's very committed to us. And we have a network of very enthusiastic supporters.' Alex had photographs of them as well, but she doubted that Leo would want to see them.

He nodded. 'And you have your own office?'

'Yes. It's a loft room. The law firm that owns the building wasn't using it and they let us have it free of charge.'

'That's good of them. And what do you do for them in return?' His eyes seemed to bore into her, both tempting and cajoling at the same time.

'The senior partner's son takes part in one of our training programmes.'

'And this boy—he fulfils your standard criteria for this service?'

Anger seized hold of her. Alex knew the exact position of the photograph in the pile, and she snatched it out, dropping it onto the table in front of Leo. 'He was born without the lower part of both legs. Like most five-year-olds, he loves running and playing football. His name is Sam.'

Leo glanced down at the photograph, his face suddenly softening. As he reached out to touch it with his fingertips, Alex saw the melting blue eyes of the young man she'd once met.

'It looks as if Sam's pretty good with that ball.'

'He is. What he doesn't have in speed, he makes up for with tactics.'

'Well, I hope I'll get a chance to see him play.' It was just a glimpse of compassion—a brief acknowledgement that Leo really did understand what Together Our Way was all about. But it was enough to stop Alex from giving up on him completely and putting her involvement in this project up for review.

And then the moment was gone. The tea arrived, and Leo took that as a cue to resume his questioning. The way the charity was run. Exactly what they spent their money on. How many volunteers they had, how they dealt with Health and Safety. He was nothing if not thorough and, although Alex struggled to keep up with him, he seemed content with her answers.

'And now that I know all about you—' his smile became melting again '—it brings me to the question of 2KZ's planned involvement.'

Maybe he'd been a little hard on her. There was actually no maybe about it, but Alex hadn't let him walk all over her and Leo respected that. And the delicious surprise of seeing her again…

Had been shockingly tempered when he realised that she had been through so much in the last ten years. An accident, losing her leg. But she'd turned that around. And, out of respect for her, he'd concentrated on her achievements.

If it had been anyone else, he would have allowed the personal to oil the wheels of the professional. But Alex clearly didn't want to put their relationship on that level. She hadn't called him back ten years ago. And even though she'd known it was him, she'd left it to her assistant to call him and arrange this meeting. Leo wasn't prone to holding grudges, but that looked like a pretty definite expression of intent.

He'd reacted like an iceman, shrinking from a flame. Ill-prepared, because of an emergency with one of the patients at his GP's surgery, he'd asked the questions he needed to ask and kept his feelings to himself.

And his feelings weren't a part of this equation. If Together Our Way was slightly amateurish in its approach, its heart was quite definitely in the right place. It was an organisation that his show could make a big difference to, and Leo seldom turned down a challenge.

'As I said, the spotlight we're proposing is a little different from the one first offered.' This was the sticking point. 'The intention now is that I'll be hosting a representative from Together Our Way as a guest on my medical phone-in show, once a week during the whole of February. I'm assuming that it will be you?'

Panic flared in her eyes, and Leo felt another little piece of him melt in response. Clearly the idea that she'd be talking live on the radio hadn't registered with Alex the first time he'd mentioned it.

But she rallied beautifully. 'Yes. It'll be me.'

'I'm trying to get some ten or fifteen minute slots on our Community Affairs programme in addition to that. That'll involve me spending some time with you, and seeing your work first-hand. I assume you have no objections to that?'

'We'd welcome it. What do you have in mind?'

'I'll be making reports, and probably writing a few articles for our website. And there'll be an outside broadcast...' He fell silent. He could see from her face that Alex had an issue with that, and he waited for her to put it into words.

'Would you be happy to fit in with our way of doing things? Our first priority is the young people we serve, and if we needed to change that emphasis to accommodate you we'd have some difficulty.'

She'd have no *difficulty* in changing; she just wasn't prepared to do it. Good for her. 'We'd be there to observe. Low-profile isn't my usual approach, so I'll be giving those muscles a little much-needed exercise.'

Her pursed lips reminded him of a severe version of a kiss. 'That's part of what we do. Help exercise under-used muscles.'

'We'll stay flexible, then.' He imagined that Alex was just as used to acting on her own initiative as he was, and that might be interesting. Even so, it was time to flex the muscles he *did* use regularly and remind her who was in charge of this project.

'2KZ has broadcast to the whole of London for more than thirty years now. Interviews with young people appeal to our listeners and we know how to do them appropriately and with all the necessary safeguards and permissions. We give our listeners what they want, and outside broadcasts are very good for ratings.'

Another disapproving look. Maybe he needed to mention that ratings weren't just a number on a spreadsheet; they represented hearts and minds. She might deal in hearts and minds but she couldn't reach them without his domination of the ratings lists.

Despite all that disapproval, she came to the right decision. 'That sounds excellent. As long as our young people are properly supported and safeguarded, I think an outside broadcast would certainly be something we'd be keen to do.'

'Good. Anything else?'

'Yes, would you mind if we featured the spotlight on our website?'

'We'd welcome it. We can provide you with artwork if that's of any help. I'll have our in-house designer get in touch with… You have a web designer?'

'That's me, actually.' She shrugged. 'I'm afraid it's not very professional. One of those standard template designs…'

He'd looked at her website briefly and had been very favourably impressed. 'If you like, I can set up a call with our designer. She's got a lot of experience with liaising with other organisations we partner with, and a conversation might be helpful.'

'Thank you. I'd be grateful for any suggestions she has.' Alex paused, squeezing her hands together. She seemed to have something else on her mind.

'If there are any other issues, now's the time to raise them. We have a very tight schedule on this.'

'I've never been on the radio before…' And she was clearly terrified at the prospect.

'That's what I'm there for. I ask a few questions, to steer things in the right direction, and step in when you dry up…'

He couldn't help smiling when Alex's eyebrows shot up. 'Everyone dries up first time. It's expected.'

'Right. I'll try not to do it too much.'

'Be yourself. Don't think about it too much; just say what you want to say. There's a seven second broadcast delay, which allows us to catch anything too bad before it airs. It's supposed to be so that we can cut any profanity, but it works pretty well if you suddenly find you've forgotten what you were about to say.'

'I won't forget. This is really important to me, and I want to do it well.'

Leo nodded, taking a sip of his tea. 'That's exactly what I wanted to hear. Hold that thought and you'll be fine.'

He seemed to have loosened up a bit, which was good, because the giddy chicane of Leo's questioning, and his efficient, autocratic way of doing things, had left her almost weak with exhaustion. He took a thick card from his jacket pocket and handed it to her.

'Here's my number. I dare say that our PR department will be bombarding you with all kinds of details that don't really matter. If you want to cut through all of that, give me a call.'

Alex looked at the card. It was printed with Leo's name and a mobile phone number. She'd never met anyone who had personal calling cards before. 'Thank you. But I don't want to bother you…'

'You won't be. It's always better to sort things out direct, and we don't have any time for messing about.' His gaze raked her face but he said nothing more. Perhaps he'd called her, ten years ago. Maybe she should explain why she hadn't called back, but Alex couldn't think of a tactful way to approach that conversation.

'Yes. Thank you. Can I give you my number?' Alex rummaged in her bag and found the box of cards with the charity's contact details, scribbling her own name and mobile number on the back and handing it to him.

'Thank you.' He glanced at the card and put it in his pocket, seeming to relax a little now that the business of the afternoon had been despatched. 'It's good to see you again, Alex. If I'd known it was you, I'd have come in costume...'

'Then I'd have had to do the same.'

His lips twitched into a smile. Pure, seductive charm, which rushed straight to her head. 'That would have been the one and only thing which would have persuaded me to leave home looking so outrageously foolish.'

Alex had rather liked outrageously foolish. Clearly Leo didn't any more.

'It's just as well you didn't know, then.'

She grabbed her bag, wondering if she was supposed to leave now, and he stood immediately. Leo was done with her now, and about to move on to the next thing on his agenda.

It wasn't until she was walking away that Alex realised that there was one thing he hadn't asked, one thing he hadn't done. Her CV stated quite clearly that losing the lower part of her right leg in a car accident and her subsequent rehabilitation had inspired her to study physiotherapy and then to found Together Our Way. But, even though his questions had been searching and thorough, he hadn't brought the subject up, nor had his eyes wandered to where the prosthesis was hidden beneath the fabric of her trousers.

She should be pleased. Alex sometimes had to struggle to get people to see past her accident and the loss of her leg, and that was exactly what Leo had done. It was chastening, though. He might have remembered her, but it seemed he cared so little about her that he hadn't even mentioned it.

Leo watched her go, wondering if the tremble of his limbs was some kind of delayed shock. The last time she'd walked away from him, he hadn't seen her for another ten years.

He had no doubt that this time would be different, but he still couldn't help feeling that he wanted to call after her.

But running after Alex was a very bad idea. She was committed and clever, and the amount she'd achieved in the last ten years was nothing short of extraordinary. When she smiled at him the warmth in her eyes was mesmerising, reflecting all the possibilities that he no longer had it in his heart to believe in. Ten years ago, he'd been as much in love with her as it was possible to be after only one night together, but now love wasn't on his agenda.

The memory of the night they'd met, the dizzy rush of blood to his head, the tingle as all his senses went into overdrive, almost overwhelmed him. But all that was in the past. He just couldn't contemplate a relationship, that bond that required his full commitment, his full attention.

He looked at his watch and signalled to the waiter for the bill. He'd have to leave now, if he wasn't going to be late for his next appointment.

Leo stood, stretching his limbs. There really was no choice about this. If he pulled out, then 2KZ had no other suitable applicants who could respond at such short notice. If she pulled out, then Together Our Way would lose a golden opportunity to increase public awareness about their work. And if his association with Alex didn't look as if it was going to be all plain sailing, then he'd deal with that as it happened.

CHAPTER THREE

LEO KEPT HIS PROMISES. A letter, confirming what they'd discussed, arrived at her office the next morning. When the negotiations over the outside broadcast had stalled, he had called and spoken to Alex about it, then gone away and sorted the whole thing out within ten minutes. He was perceptive, intelligent and he made things happen.

She listened to his radio show without fail, telling herself that the sound of Leo's voice was an incidental pleasure and that preparing herself for what was to come was the real object. The on-air version of Leo was slightly different from the one she'd met, still astute and probing but not so confrontational, his gentle charm putting people at ease and encouraging them to talk.

Afraid to trust in either the public face or the private one, she left most of the liaison to Rhona, picking up her normal duties in return. Two weeks, a week—and then there was no avoiding it. Everything was arranged, and the following Monday saw the first of her guest appearances on the Dr Leo Cross medical phone-in show.

Alex had arrived at the radio station at six, two hours before the show was due to start. Half an hour had been taken up with a short induction from one of the production assistants, and then she'd been taken to an empty studio to have a look around. Leo was due to arrive at seven, but Alex was reliably informed that he was always late.

'What are you reading?' She'd given up looking at her watch and was sitting alone in the restroom, trying to read, when she heard Leo's voice.

'Oh… It's the latest thing apparently, for teenagers.' She tilted the cover towards him and he nodded. 'I like to keep up. It's actually pretty good.'

He smiled, and suddenly warmth zinged in the air between them. He was dressed in jeans and a dark blue sweater that looked far too soft to be anything other than cashmere. However hard Alex tried to look at him dispassionately, he still took her breath away.

He slung a leather jacket down onto a chair and sat down. 'How are you feeling? Nervous?'

Sick with nerves. That must be probably pretty obvious. 'A little…'

'You'll be fine. Once we get started, the hour will go too fast and you'll be wanting more time.' He was leaning towards her, his elbows on his knees. This was clearly Leo's pep talk for beginners and, strangely, it seemed to be working. Now that the dreaded time had come, and he was here, she felt better about everything.

'So… What are we going to say?'

Leo shrugged. 'No idea. I'll introduce you, we'll take a few calls and we'll talk. That's the thing about phone-in radio—there's no script.'

'You like that? The uncertainty?'

He grinned. 'Yeah. Keeps me on my toes. You'll be just great, trust me. And if you're not, then I'll just interrupt and steer things back on course.'

'Right. Thanks.' She'd rather be just great, and not need Leo to save the day. But then that might be a bit too much to ask on her first time.

The door burst open and Alex jumped as the production assistant who'd showed her around popped her head around the door. 'Leo… Fifteen minutes.'

'Okay, thanks. We're ready.' He turned to Alex as the

door closed again. 'Just relax. It's a conversation between you and me. Concentrate on that, and the one person out there who's listening.'

'One person?'

'Yeah. Just visualise someone you know, and talk to them. You'll be surprised how well that works.'

'I'll try.' Alex wondered who Leo visualised. Maybe he'd been doing this long enough not to need anyone. 'Was it this nerve-racking for you? Your first time?'

He shook his head. 'Nah. I didn't have any nerves left to be racked. I was so numb with fear that you could have knocked me over the head with a brick and I probably wouldn't have noticed. And I wasn't tipped in at the deep end, like you. I'd been volunteering on a student helpline for years, and done some spots on local radio in connection with that.'

'That must have been pretty tough. Manning a helpline at the same time as you were studying and working at the hospital.' Leo hadn't said anything about a helpline ten years ago, and Alex had thought they'd talked about almost everything in their lives.

'It was something that meant a lot to me. You make time for the things that are important.' His face seemed to harden a little, as if the memory was difficult.

'And you've stayed here. Even though you're on TV now.' It seemed a little odd that he should hang on to this, when he obviously had other opportunities. Leo didn't seem the type for sentimentality.

'Yeah. I like talking to people.' He shook his head, as if to clear it, and then grinned. 'You'll see.'

He ushered her through to the studio, giving her time to get settled. The producer hurried in, putting a few sheets of paper in front of him, and then the call for silence and the 'On-Air' light glowed red.

She hardly heard the music that heralded the start of the show, hardly saw what was going on around her. Then she felt Leo's fingers brush the back of her hand. His gaze caught hers and he smiled, then started the introduction.

'And tonight I have Alex Jackson with me. She's the founder of Together Our Way, a charity which helps young people with all kinds of disabilities participate in sport…' He glanced down at the paper the producer had put in front of him and frowned suddenly. 'Alex is going to be on the line with me here, and so if you've got any questions for her then you know the number to call…'

The jingle for the phone number started to play and Leo took the opportunity to scrunch up the paper in front of him, tossing it towards the control room. It bounced off the glass and dropped to the floor and then suddenly, seamlessly, Leo was talking again.

'To start us all off, I'm going to ask Alex a few questions about Together Our Way. And, just in case anyone accuses me of monopolising her time here, she will be right here with me every Monday for the next four weeks, as part of our Charity Partnership Project…'

Suddenly his gaze was on her. The smile on his lips, the look in his eyes, said that he was talking just to her. 'Alex, how long since you founded your charity…?'

He'd given her an easy one to start with. 'Five years.'

'And in that time you've made yourselves felt. How many sports fixtures are you planning next month?'

'We have eight. But our own sports meetings are just the tip of the iceberg. We've been working with schools and clubs, advising them on how their sport can be fully inclusive, and we've developed a training day for group leaders. Mostly, though, we work with the young people themselves, to help…'

Suddenly, her mind went blank.

'I imagine that there's a bit of confidence-building to be done.' Leo's eyes were suddenly warm and soothing, dark as a blue Mediterranean sea.

'Yes, that's right. Many of our young people need assistance with special equipment or training, but it's also a matter of showing everyone what's possible.'

'So you're out to capture hearts and minds?' Somehow, he made it seem as if it was *his* heart and *his* mind that were the ones in question and that they were just waiting to be captured.

'Yes. I think that's the aim of any charity, isn't it? Money's vital to us, of course, because we couldn't do what we do without it. But hearts and minds are just as important.'

'And I see that the charity's run on a shoestring, so all the donations you receive go straight into your work.'

He was feeding her lines, bringing up all the points that Alex wanted to highlight. She smiled a thank you. 'Yes, that's right…'

Alex felt as if she'd run a marathon. It had only been an hour, but she was exhausted, her heart thumping in her chest. All the same, Leo had been right. She was eager for more, and had been disappointed when he'd announced that this was all they had time for tonight and handed over to the next presenter.

'Did we speak to everyone?' Leo had said that there were callers waiting but Alex had been unable to gauge how many, or whether they'd been able to speak to them all.

'There are always people who don't get through. Some of them try again.' Now that they were off-air, Leo seemed suddenly more guarded.

'But… They may be in trouble. They might need some-one to talk to…'

'Yeah, a lot of them do. We have procedures to deal with that. You needn't worry about that side of things.'

She couldn't—wouldn't—let him give her the brush-off like this. 'I'm… I'm sorry Leo, but that's not the answer I'd hoped for.'

Alex was expecting some kind of reaction; Leo clearly

wasn't used to being challenged by anyone around here. But she hadn't expected a smile.

'What answer were you hoping for, then?'

She took a deep breath. 'That there's some way that I could get back to the people who didn't get through.'

He leaned forward, flipping a switch on the console in front of him. Alex's headphones went dead and she realised that, even though the sound engineer in the control room seemed to be paying no attention to it, their conversation could be overheard. She slipped the headset off and laid it down.

'The call-handlers take names and numbers from everyone, and they always ask what the caller wants to say.'

'And they make a note of that?'

'Yes, they do. And they pass the list on to me.' That seemed to be the end of it as far as Leo was concerned. *He* was the trustworthy one, the one who got things done, and he was ready to steamroller over anyone who questioned him.

Maybe she'd deserved it. Maybe he *had* called her all those years ago, and he still remembered that she hadn't called him back.

'Look, Leo. I think there's something… We need to clear something up.'

'What would that be?'

He gave so little. It was questions all the way with Leo, and she was starting to wonder whether he wasn't hiding behind them.

'Did you call me after the party?' Alex wondered how he'd like a taste of his own medicine, and answered his question with one of her own.

He seemed surprised. 'I'm not sure I remember.'

'Why don't you try?' If this issue was getting in the way of the work she was committed to now, she wanted an answer.

'I said I would.' His slight shrug seemed designed to

imply that it really didn't matter all that much to him. 'But that's the way it works. It's a lady's privilege not to call back.'

He flashed her his most charming, roguish smile. That alone probably made the chances of any woman not calling him back extremely slim. Or maybe it was just Leo's way of changing the subject.

'Since you won't give me a straight answer, I'll assume that you *did* call. And I've been wanting to tell you that I'm sorry I didn't get back to you, but I really couldn't. Something happened on the way home and…it was impossible.'

She had his full attention now. Leo couldn't hide the surprise in his eyes. 'What happened?'

'I…' Alex gulped. It was all such a long time ago now and it ought to be irrelevant, but it wasn't. A rap sounded on the glass that separated them from the control room and she jumped.

'I'm sorry.' Leo snapped suddenly into professional mode. 'The producer's here, and I need to have a word with him. Would you mind waiting?'

Alex nodded and he swung to his feet, striding to the door and closing it behind him. He reappeared on the other side of the glass, where a man was waiting for him.

Leo's back was turned to her but the man was glancing at her, even though Leo was obviously talking to him. Curiosity got the better of Alex and she reached for her headphones, flipping the switch that she now knew controlled the sound between the control room and the studio.

'It's not acceptable, Justin.' Leo's voice rang in her ears.

'I really don't see what the problem is…' Alex saw Justin spread his hands in a gesture of puzzlement.

'Well, there isn't any problem because I'm not going to do it. I won't introduce Alex Jackson as a *disabled person*. She has a disability, and she's open about that, but I'm not going to read out an introduction that makes it seem as if it's the most important thing about her. She's here to talk about her charity, which, by the way, is all about encouraging young people to see past their disabilities. *And* educating others to do that too.'

Alex's gaze moved to the screwed up ball of paper on the floor, which Leo had tossed at the glass. He'd moved past it so smoothly that she'd hardly realised he had a problem with it.

'Okay…okay.' Justin's tone was conciliatory. 'It was an error of emphasis, I'll grant you that. No harm done, though…'

'Only because I didn't read the introduction out. I want to hear all the trailers for the show, because I don't want Alex or her charity misrepresented.'

This was almost too much. Leo was fighting her corner without being asked, but just knowing how she'd feel. A thrill of warmth for him clutched at her heart and Alex wondered whether she should go and retrieve the paper, to see what had been written. But then she'd have to take the headphones off, and she wanted to hear this.

'We'll email the sound files through to you. Anything else?'

'No. I'm grateful you're addressing the issue with your customary effectiveness.' Leo's tone had relaxed into lazy charm. 'Actually, there is one more thing. Thanks for all you did to help make this evening happen. It's been a good night.'

Justin seemed to heave a sigh of relief. 'Yep. Nice chemistry in there, Leo. And the caller rate went through the roof…' Justin's gaze flipped towards Alex and Leo turned. When he saw her, his lip curled imperceptibly.

She reddened and took off the headphones, putting them back onto the console. Perhaps he'd think she was just trying them on.

Leo had followed Justin out of the control room and when he appeared at the door of the studio again he was holding a manila envelope.

'Your car's waiting.'

And he thought he was going to slip away now? 'No, Leo. I'm not going anywhere until we finish…what we were talking about.'

'I thought I'd catch a lift with you. The car's a lot more private.' He walked across to the console and, too late, Alex realised that she'd forgotten to cut the sound in between the control room and the studio, and that voices were whispering out of the headphones.

He reached out, switching the sound off again. Then he turned, leaving Alex to grab her coat and handbag and follow him out of the studio.

Leo wondered whether letting sleeping dogs lie was the best option. It probably was, but he knew that wasn't what he was going to do. Not many people questioned his decisions and, while it came as no surprise that Alex bucked that trend, it was unexpectedly like a breath of fresh air.

She settled herself on the wide leather seat in the back of the car, and Leo got in beside her. The driver confirmed the address with her and the car slid smoothly out onto the road.

'This is nice.' She stretched her legs out in front of her, smiling. Clearly she was attempting to disarm him before she started on the next onslaught. He wondered briefly if she knew how much damage her smile could do to a man.

The lights from the street outside were sliding across her face, giving it an almost ethereal quality and it was an effort to stop himself from staring at her. Alex was even more perfect than when he'd first met her. Or maybe he'd just become more of a connoisseur of perfection and learned how to appreciate it better.

He pressed the control button and the glass partition behind the driver's seat slid upwards. Not that the driver probably cared two hoots about their conversation, but the gesture wasn't lost on Alex and her cheeks reddened.

'What happened?' It was probably something stupid—she'd lost her phone or met an old boyfriend on the bus. But Leo had learned the hard way that hoping for the best didn't always mean that the best was going to happen. He had to be sure.

She ignored the question. That usually annoyed him, but Alex did it so blatantly that the assertive twist of her mouth was enchanting.

'I want to thank you. For standing up for me... I mean the charity. And our aims.'

'That's what a good host does.'

'I know. But it doesn't always happen, and... Thank you. You're a very good host.'

People said that all the time, but on her lips the compliment warmed him. Despite that, he still hadn't forgotten what he wanted to ask her...

'What happened? On your way home.'

'I had an accident. I lost my phone.'

'What kind of accident?' Something tingled at the back of Leo's neck. That instinct, honed over years of listening to people, told him that whatever she was about to say next was important.

'I got off the bus and crossed the road...' She paused for a moment, as if the memory was a difficult one.

Leo was trying not to put two and two together and make four. Hoping that the almost inevitable conclusion wasn't the right one, this time.

'And...?'

'I was knocked over by a car. Drunk driver. I woke up in hospital and my phone was... I don't know where it was. It was gone.'

A great wave of horror seemed suspended above his head, just waiting to crash down on him. 'This was...' He couldn't even say it. His finger twitched, gesturing towards her right leg.

'Yes. My right foot and the lower part of my leg were

completely crushed. The only way I'd ever be able to walk again, or be pain free, was for them to amputate below the knee.'

The full horror of it washed over him in a suffocating wall of guilt and remorse. 'Alex… I'm so sorry. If I'd known…'

'You couldn't have known.'

All he could think about was the trail of small events which had ended in this one great one. If he'd only done just one thing differently…

'I should have seen you home.' He remembered that he'd offered and that she'd told him no. If only he'd insisted. If they'd even just argued about it, and she'd missed her bus and had to wait for the next one…

'What would you have done? There were witnesses and they said that the car swerved right across the road and hit me. There was no getting out of the way.'

'I might have helped…somehow.' Anyhow. If all he could have done was just hold her hand, then he would have done it with every ounce of his strength. But he hadn't been there for Alex, and then six months later he hadn't been there for his brother either. The thought seemed to be literally eating at him, taking great chunks of his flesh and leaving him quivering with shock.

Her gaze searched his face. 'You would have put me back together again? That was beyond anyone.'

He couldn't answer. Didn't have words to tell her how sorry he was—for all she'd been through, and for his part in it.

'Do me a favour, eh?' Her voice was soft and he felt her fingers brush his arm. Clawing him back from the memories that swirled in his head.

'Yeah?' Anything.

'I've given up on the *what if* because the past can't be changed. I prefer to concentrate on *what is*.' She shot him an imploring look. 'Please…'

It was an effort to smile, but if Alex could do it so could he. 'You've got it.'

There was one thing he could do. The only thing that made him feel any better about having let his brother down were the people he could help now. Leo guarded that role jealously, never letting anyone else get in the way, and no one ever asked about the call-backs that he made after each show. But Alex had.

He slid the manila envelope across the seat towards her.

'What's this?' She touched it lightly with her fingers, seeming to know that it was something important.

'It's the list of people who didn't get through to the show. Names, numbers and I ask the call-handlers to find out whether they would like a return call if they don't get through.'

'And you were going to tell me about this?' She narrowed her eyes.

'I don't usually volunteer the information. But you did ask.' The envelope lay between them, Alex's fingers at one end of it and his at the other. As if neither of them could quite bring themselves to let go.

'So…when were you thinking of calling back?'

'The call-handlers have told everyone that it'll be tomorrow, late afternoon. I have a surgery in the morning but I'm usually finished by about three o'clock.'

She nodded. 'If you want a hand… Actually, I think I'm going to insist on helping.'

He felt his lips curl into a smile. 'You're free tomorrow afternoon?'

'Yes. I usually work Wednesday to Friday at the hospital, but I'm taking some time off over the next few weeks. I can be available any time.'

He was suddenly almost breathless. It was as if they were making a tryst. More than that, because this would require his full attention.

'You'll be at your office? I can come to you, and we'll go through the list together.'

'That sounds good. Although you might like to bring a scarf. The heating's on the blink again.'

'Sounds delightful. I'll be there at about half past three.' He pushed the envelope another inch towards her. There was a copy back at the radio station, but it still felt difficult to give it up. 'You take this. But don't call anyone until I get there...'

She grinned, stowing the envelope in her bag. 'I imagine they've been told that they'll be hearing from you, not me. Don't worry, I'll wait.'

Before he got the chance to change his mind, the car drew up outside a block of solidly built flats, set back from the road behind a curving drive. Leo made to get out and she laid her hand on his arm.

'I think I can make it on my own.'

She knew just what he'd been thinking, and Leo jumped guiltily. He'd made the promise, but it still wasn't easy to stop thinking about all the things that might happen to her in between here and her front door. 'I dare say you can. But...'

Alex chuckled. 'I know. A gentleman always sees a lady to her door.' She got out of the car, bending down before closing the door. 'I'm no lady. I'll see you tomorrow.'

Leo begged to disagree. He watched her as she smiled at the driver, giving him a wave and a nod of thanks. She was every inch a lady.

'Wait...' The instruction was unnecessary, as their driver seemed as unwilling to go before Alex was safely inside as he was. She opened the main door and then turned, flapping her hand as if to shoo them away, and, without any reference to him at all, the car pulled out onto the road.

Leo kicked the door closed behind him. The car had retraced its route, driving back into town to the flat that he kept for weekdays, ten minutes' walk from the radio station.

The flat was quiet and dark, shadows slanting across the floor. He fixed himself a drink and, without taking his coat off, slid back the large windows and walked out onto the roof terrace, set seventeen floors above the ground and commanding a view across practically the whole of London. Alex was out there somewhere. One of the lights shimmering in the distance was hers.

He moved closer to the glass barriers which stood at the perimeter of the terrace and a gust of chilly air hit him full in the face. Leo shivered. He had no right to wonder what she was doing, or to wish that he could be doing it with her.

Leo Cross. Never there when you needed him.

He hadn't been there for Alex. To the extent that he hadn't even known that she'd needed him. But he'd known that his brother needed him. He'd known that Joel was under stress, that his first job after university hadn't turned out quite the way he'd wanted it, but Joel had seemed a lot better, and promised Leo that he was handling it. Leo had returned from a weekend away to find that his brother hadn't been handling it at all.

His father had been waiting for him, gently breaking the news that they'd lost Joel. An overdose of prescription drugs. Maybe it had been a mistake.

Leo had doubted that. Joel was his twin, and he knew him almost better than he knew himself. And when he'd finally been able to get a couple of moments alone he'd found the missed calls on his phone. Joel had called him on that Saturday evening.

The brothers used to joke about missed calls. Once meant: *I'll catch you later.* Twice: *Call me back.* Three times: *Call me back now.* The five missed calls on Leo's phone had spoken to him loud and clear. *I'm in trouble. I need you, Leo...*

He pulled his phone from his pocket, scanning it. There

was a text from his mother, saying she'd heard the show tonight, and automatically he hit speed dial.

'Hi, Mum…' Leo smiled into the phone, knowing that even if it was forced, the smile would sound in his voice. 'How are you doing?'

'Oh, darling! Exhausted. I went shopping with Marjorie today…'

'Yeah? Find anything nice?'

'Of course we did. You know Marjorie. I heard the programme tonight.'

His mother could always be relied on to give him an honest assessment of his performance. 'What did you think?'

'Good. Very good. I was very impressed by that young woman…'

'Alex?'

'Yes. She sounds as if she's a force to be reckoned with.'

'She is. She's very committed.'

'That came over. And she sounds nice with it.'

'Yeah. She's nice too.' Leo took a sip of his Scotch.

'Pretty?'

'No. More beautiful, I'd say.' Leo chuckled. His mother's wish to see him settled down with a nice girl, preferably one he *hadn't* met at some glitzy party, was never all that far from the surface.

'That's nice. And she'll be back next week, will she?'

'You were listening, then…' Leo laughed as his mother protested. He knew well enough that she always listened. 'In which case you'll know that we're holding quite a few events over the next couple of weeks.'

'Well, I hope you enjoy them. What's that funny noise…?'

'Wind, probably. I'm on the terrace.'

'What on earth for? You'll catch your death of cold…'

'I just wanted to clear my head. I'm going inside now.'

Leo had accepted that, faced with the loss of one son, his mother could be a little over-protective about the remaining one. The least he could do was go along with it; there was little enough else he could do to ease his parents' agony. Apart from keeping quiet about the five missed calls. If his parents wanted to believe that Joel's death had been some kind of horrendous accident then he couldn't rip that shred of comfort away from them.

He slid the balcony doors closed with a bump and threw himself down onto the sofa.

'You sound tired, darling.'

'Long day. I'm about ready to turn in now.'

'Well, don't let me stop you. Goodnight.'

'Yeah. Speak soon, Mum.'

Leo ended the call, staring for a moment at the screen of his phone. Joel's number was still on there, transferred from one phone to another, over the years. It was stupid, really, but it reminded him why he did what he did. Why the radio show was so important to him. He hadn't been around to help Joel, and the only thing that made that agony a little easier to bear was the hope that maybe, as a result of something he'd done, there was another family out there who hadn't had to grieve the way his had.

And now Alex. He'd let her down, as surely as he'd let Joel down. But there was one very big difference. There was no possibility of going back and helping Joel. But Alex… She had a future, and he could do something to change that.

Putting his glass down on the small table beside the sofa, he walked into the bedroom, picking up the key to the gym downstairs. Hard physical work would calm his mind and help him think straight. And he needed some ideas about how exactly he was going to make things up to Alex.

CHAPTER FOUR

DESPITE HAVING VOWED that Leo was going to have to take the office as he found it, Alex had been working hard since lunchtime, tidying and vacuuming the small space, cleaning the windows and putting the two most comfortable chairs on either side of her desk. Rhona was working at home today and she had the place to herself.

Her thick sweater and sheepskin boots were just about keeping the cold at bay, but she couldn't expect Leo to freeze. When she left the office door open, some of the heat from downstairs percolated upwards and the electric heater in the corner was making some difference. By four o'clock it might be warm enough to think about taking her scarf off.

Finally, she put the envelope on her desk, still sealed. She'd wanted to look inside, but wanted even more to show Leo that she understood that he'd trusted her, and that she'd taken that seriously. Sitting down, she surveyed her handiwork. The place didn't look too bad at all. Apart from Rhona's mug… Alex got to her feet, grabbing the mug from the tray and hiding it in her desk drawer. Leo didn't need to come face to face with a row of stick figures demonstrating the fourteen most popular positions from the *Kama Sutra*.

'You call this accessible?' He appeared suddenly in the doorway, tall and lean, dressed in jeans and a heavy sweater under his jacket.

'No. We call it cheap.' She returned his grin. He must have walked straight past the receptionist downstairs, found his way to the lift and then up the flight of narrow stairs on his own. Breezing in as if he owned the place seemed to come as second nature to Leo.

'I brought provisions.' He set a brown paper carrier bag down on the desk.

Alex peered into the bag and drew out a large polystyrene container, peeling back the lid. 'Don't tell me you made this yourself.'

He chuckled. 'What do you think I am? Of course I didn't; I stopped off at a place I know.'

'Who just happen to do the best French onion soup in town?' It smelled gorgeous.

'Debatable. They're in the running, but tell me what you think.'

She fetched paper napkins for the crusty, fresh baked bread and Leo tore open the manila envelope. They reviewed the list while they ate.

'That's a good question...' She tapped the paper with her finger. 'I should have said a bit more about how we weight our races so that everyone has a fair chance.'

'He's a regular caller. I'd be surprised if he doesn't call again next Monday; I'll let the call-handlers know we want to talk to him.'

'Can you do that?' Alex had supposed that everyone just waited in line.

'We do it all the time. It's a radio show; we balance the calls to provide the best broadcast we can...' He caught sight of Alex's frown of disappointment. 'Don't do that to me.'

'What?'

'That disapproving face. Look, I know what you're thinking...'

'No, you don't.'

In the sudden silence, Alex could hear the chair creak as

Leo leaned back in it. 'You're thinking that this is all about heightening awareness and reaching people who need the service you offer. Not about making good listening while people do the washing-up.'

That was exactly what she was thinking. Maybe not quite in those words; Leo had put it much more succinctly than she could have done. 'And if I was thinking that?'

'If you were, I'd tell you that my world's different from yours. For me, it has to be all about ratings, and making sure that the show's popular enough to survive. Being realistic is what makes me good at what I do.'

Why did he have to do this? Every time Leo did something nice, he devalued it, pretended that it was all self-serving. Or maybe he was just being honest. Maybe she was just looking for something in him that was no longer there.

'So you're really just a cynic?' He wasn't. She knew he wasn't, or what would he be doing here, calling people back? Why had he guarded the list so jealously?

'Yeah.'

'I don't believe you.' Alex felt herself redden.

'That's because you're an idealist.' He reached into his jacket pocket, pulling out his phone and propping it on the desk between them. 'Which is what makes you so good at what *you* do, and exactly why you're the best person to help me with these calls.'

Perhaps he'd gone a little too far. Alex had seemed ready to shake him, until she heard what she wanted to hear. But that wasn't what Leo was prepared to give.

It would be so easy, so very pleasurable, to indulge the connection between them. To reach out and touch her, knowing that their hearts weren't so very different. He wanted that, and he had a good idea that Alex did too, but if he felt her softness he'd be unable to stop.

He'd been this way before, and recognised the signposts. Love affairs which bloomed briefly and then faded, as it became all too obvious that even when Leo was physically present, his mind was elsewhere. In the end, he had resigned himself to the fact that short-cutting the process, and keeping his relationships with women strictly on the level of a friendship, saved a lot of heartache all round.

A love affair with Alex might be very sweet, but it would inevitably be short. And Leo needed time. Time to help her dreams for the charity come to fruition. He was there to be used, and the sooner he convinced her that he owed her that, the better.

She didn't press her point. Almost as soon as he'd dialled the first number, she was smiling again, ready to talk. He grinned at her, leaning over to speak into the phone.

'Hello... This is Leo Cross. Is that Nina?'

There was a long pause. 'Yes...'

'You called my radio show yesterday evening, about your nephew, John. He has cerebral palsy, and you'd like to know what opportunities there are for him to play football.' It was always good to give people a few details, just to reassure them that this wasn't a hoax call. 'I have Alex Jackson with me...'

'You do?'

Alex leaned over towards the phone. 'Hi, Nina.'

'Leo... Thank you for calling. I didn't think you would. I'd love to talk...'

'We're here to listen. Tell us about John...'

It had taken three hours to work their way through the list. Longer than usual, but then last night's show had been popular. Alex had done most of the talking, and Leo had taken the opportunity to watch her. She didn't so much speak into his phone, but shone into it. He wondered whether little trails of light would leak back out of it when they were done and he put the phone back into his pocket.

'Last one?' She consulted the list. 'What does that star by her name mean?'

'Under eighteen. Look, it says she's seventeen.'

'Right. But she's old enough to consult someone medically on her own if she wants to.'

'Yep, but not necessarily on the radio. We need parental consent for under sixteens, and if they're sixteen to eighteen we have an extra duty of care.'

Alex nodded, grinning. 'So let's fast-track this one. I'll get stroppy about a seventeen-year-old calling a phone-in show because she needs help and then not getting to speak to anyone. You'll tell me you have some kind of procedure and she's been well looked after. Then I feel like an idiot.'

'She'll have spoken to a counsellor. But you're not an idiot.' Alex's stubborn belief in him was beginning to grow on Leo, and it was becoming harder to cling to the reasons why he shouldn't believe in himself.

'That's that dealt with then. She's definitely a pink.' Alex had used pink highlighter for follow-ups, green for everyone who hadn't requested a call, and yellow for those who'd raised important issues that she'd like to talk about on the next programme. The list was beginning to resemble a Neapolitan ice cream, and Leo wondered whether Alex would like the Italian ice cream parlour in Knightsbridge. He saved that thought carefully as he dialled the mobile phone number.

'Hi, this is Leo Cross. Is that Carys?'

Alex had leaned in a little closer to the phone with each call they made. This time her hair brushed his cheek, and Leo shivered. The sound of an alarmed squawk came from the phone, and when they both jumped he caught the faint but alluring scent of her perfume.

'Carys…?' It was an effort to keep his voice steady.

A pause, the sound of a TV in the background.

'I can't talk…' The words were whispered down the line.

'Okay, that's fine. Would you like to talk another time?'

'Yes. Please… I want to…'

The hairs on the back of Leo's neck prickled. He'd

worked on helplines for long enough to know when someone really wanted to talk, and he guessed that the girl needed to do so in private.

'What time's good for you, Carys?' Leo looked at his watch. 'Would you like me to call you in an hour?'

'Yes. Thanks.'

'That's no problem. I'll call you at eight, and if I don't get through to you I'll try again tomorrow.'

'Yes. Good. Thanks.'

The line cut before Leo could say anything else and he looked up into Alex's gaze.

'What do we do now?'

He smiled. It was so easy to smile into her honey-brown eyes, and when he did so he always saw some spark of a response. 'I'll wait and call her back in an hour.'

'Is that going to be okay? You're not meant to be anywhere else, are you?'

Actually, he was. The solution which presented itself curled its way around his mind, beckoning him to at least ask. 'I have a drinks party in Hampstead but if I go home now and change, then I can call Carys and then leave straight away. If you'd like to come back with me, we can talk to her together. If you're not busy tonight.'

'No... No, I've got nothing on. Are you sure that's okay?'

'It's fine. And it's starting to get cold in here anyway.' The encroaching chill of the evening was finally making itself felt, despite the portable radiator. 'I'll drop you home afterwards; it's not far out of my way.'

'If it's no trouble... It sounds as if Carys wants to talk.'

'Yeah, it does.' Leo rose from his seat, stretching. 'Let's go then.'

His car was parked outside the office on a meter. Alex was no connoisseur of cars, but this one had the kind of shine that made the paintwork seem almost liquid under the streetlights. And she recognised leather seats when she saw them.

'This is where you live?' He drove into the entrance to an underground car park, beneath a glass-clad tower block, less than half a mile from the radio station.

'Yes.' He slid into a parking bay and switched off the engine, leaning towards her slightly. 'Fast-track. You wonder why I came all the way to your place last night and then back again and I point out that we had some unfinished business to talk about and that the car was the best place to do it. You see my point, but think I'm an idiot.'

When Leo was in this mood, he couldn't fail to make her smile. 'I don't think you're an idiot.' Alex got out of the car before she could betray what she really *did* think.

The flat was gorgeous. On the top floor, the city lights spread out behind floor to ceiling windows. The seating area was designed to impress, with a huge glass-topped table between black leather sofas that were long enough to lie down, stretch right out and still not be able to touch both ends.

Red leather armchairs gave the room a pop of colour. Diamond-shaped bookshelves, where the books were stacked in a zigzag pattern, a touch of class. A huge abstract painting on one wall, swirling blues and greens, was the only thing that didn't seem to conform to rigid straight lines.

He helped her out of her coat, throwing it down on an armchair and dropping his own jacket next to it, then dumping his keys on the coffee table. Clearly the almost obsessive tidiness of the place had more to do with whoever cleaned it than it did with Leo.

'This is beautiful, Leo. What a view...'

'Yeah. I took one look out of the window and knew I had to have this place. The view's different every day, and I never tire of it.'

Alex wandered over to the window, drinking in the

panorama of London at night which lay beyond the roof terrace. 'It's wonderful. Very tidy.'

He grinned. 'I don't get much time to make a mess. I only stay here during the week, when I'm in town.'

'And at weekends?'

'I have a house down in Surrey, but it's a long drive after working in the evening. Make yourself at home.'

It wasn't that easy to make herself at home in a place that so obviously wasn't one. 'I'm torn between the view and the sofa.'

He chuckled, moving one of the red leather armchairs over to the window. 'Here. Best of both worlds. Would you like something to drink?'

'Do you have any juice?'

'I expect so. I'll look.' He turned, trekking across the enormous room to a doorway which lay at one side of it. Alex flopped down into the armchair. Leo's apartment had told her nothing about him that she didn't already know. Beautiful, well thought out and sophisticated, it betrayed no clue as to the real nature of the man who lived there.

His interior designer had told him that the space by the window was for circulating during drinks parties, and the seating area was for sitting. Leo usually conformed to those instructions but it was typical of Alex that she should sub-vert the plan within two minutes of arriving here.

He found an unopened carton of juice in the fridge and poured two glasses. Moving a side table over to where Alex was sitting, along with a chair for himself, he wondered why he'd never thought of doing this before.

She'd stripped off her heavy sweater and scarf to reveal a thick checked shirt and she was rubbing at her leg fit-fully, her hand slipped down inside her boot.

'Okay?'

'Yeah. My phantom foot itches. If I rub the other one, it usually goes away.'

She'd talked about her leg on the show, fluently and without any embarrassment. But Leo had left the subject alone when they were off-air, leaving Alex to dictate what was said. Mentioning this small detail seemed like a breakthrough of some kind. Not a big one but the beginning of some kind of trust.

'You get that a lot? Phantom pain?'

'No, just occasionally. And it's more of a sensation than a pain now.'

'And rubbing the other one works?'

'It seems to. Fools the brain into thinking you're doing something about it.' She grinned at him. 'It's a trick they taught me in rehab.'

Leo hesitated. In any other circumstance this would be crossing the line he'd drawn for himself. But if he concentrated on the medical aspect, tried to learn a little about what worked and didn't work…

'I do an outstanding foot massage.' It was just a matter of not succumbing to temptation and getting carried away.

She flushed a little, snatching her hand out of her boot. 'Outstanding sounds…a bit like overkill. A bit of a rub is enough.'

Maybe that was what friends really were for. Stopping you when you were about to rush headlong into a mistake. And right now it felt as if there was no *just* about this friendship. It had the potential to be as big and beautiful as the glittering panorama they sat beside.

He should leave her alone to rub her leg in peace if she wanted to. Leo looked at his watch. Another twenty-five minutes before they were due to call Carys, which would give him time for a shower that was cold enough to bring him to his senses. 'I'll get going, then. Are you okay here, or can I get you anything?'

She shook her head, motioning towards the window. 'No, I'm fine. I have company.'

CHAPTER FIVE

IT WAS LIKE sitting in a sparkling bubble. She could see the city below her but she couldn't hear its din. The air outside had to be freezing but she was warm and relaxed. Leo would be taking a shower around now but, in the substantial structure, she couldn't hear the sound of water running.

Just as well. She didn't want to think about him in the shower, emerging from the shower… Anything even remotely connected with showers was way out of line. The idea of his touch, let alone what a massage could do, had made her feel giddy.

Alex slipped her foot out of her boot, closing her fingers around it and rubbing gently until the phantom feeling in her other leg subsided. The high tone of a phone penetrated the wall of silence and she ignored it. Leo had kept checking his phone, seeming anxious about missing the call, and it was no surprise when the tone cut off abruptly and she heard the muffled sound of Leo's voice from the bedroom.

The conversation seemed to be taking a while. She looked at her watch. Another ten minutes before they were due to call Carys. She couldn't hear his footsteps on the thick carpet, but the sound of his voice seemed to be getting closer.

'Carys… Would you like to talk to Alex? I can pass the phone over to her if that's okay with you…?'

Alex twisted round in her chair. Carys must have picked

Leo's number up from the call he'd made earlier, and not been able to wait for him to call her back. Suddenly, the whole world seemed to tip in a dizzy, vertiginous burst of rapture.

Leo's hair was wet from the shower, spiking on the top of his head as if he'd just rubbed it hastily with a towel. Perhaps the one that was currently wound around his slim hips, and the only thing he was wearing. She'd imagined that his body was perfect, but it was so much better than that. Strong, well-muscled, with smooth tanned skin. *Perfect* would have been an understatement.

And the best thing about it was that he was entirely unaware of it. Leo was concentrating on the voice on the other end of the line, and nothing else seemed to matter to him. Innocent as the day he was born, and yet far more delicious.

'Okay. Would you like me to call you back…? Yes, I'll do it straight away and then put you on to Alex. All right…'

Leo walked over to where she was sitting, which was just as well because Alex was paralysed with something that felt suspiciously like lust. He was focusing on his phone and she took the opportunity to give him one last look. *Fabulous.* He moved so well, the right mix of control and almost animal grace.

'It's Carys. Will you have a word with her while I get dressed? She lost her leg six months ago and she needs to talk…' He switched the phone to loudspeaker and put it down on the side table next to her. Alex caught the scent of soap and skin, and swallowed hard.

Six rings and then the call went to answerphone. Leo shook his head, cursing softly. 'Come on, Carys. Answer— I know you're there…'

He bent over, stabbing the phone with his finger and redialling. He was so close, one hand on the arm of her chair, and, although she was staring at the phone, the curve of his bicep nudged into her peripheral vision. But all he seemed to care about right now was that Carys hadn't answered her phone.

The line connected and Alex heard the sound of breathing. Leo smiled into the phone.

'Hey, Carys. Thought I'd lost you for a moment there. Are you still okay to talk?' His voice was friendly, like a concerned big brother.

'Yes… Sorry…'

'No problem. I know this is hard for you. Alex is with me now, and I think it would be great if you two talked a bit.'

'I'd like that…' Carys's voice quavered down the line.

'Hi, Carys. Alex here. Thanks so much for getting in touch with us.'

'Alex…'

Carys sounded as if she was crying now, and Alex leaned in, closer to the phone.

'I was wondering if I could tell you a bit about myself.' Carys didn't answer and Alex's gaze found Leo for a moment. He nodded her on. 'Okay. I lost my right leg below the knee when I was nineteen, in a car accident. It's a lot to cope with, isn't it?'

'I feel as if…all the things I wanted to do…'

'Yeah, I know. I felt like that too. And everyone says that you can still do them, but they don't know how hard it is, do they?'

'No. I keep falling flat on my face.'

'Has your physiotherapist taught you how to fall without hurting yourself…?' Alex almost didn't notice that Leo was moving away now. She concentrated hard on the phone, listening for Carys's reply.

Leo scrubbed the towel across his head and flattened his hair with a comb, then reached for his clothes. Dark trousers, a dress shirt. He'd leave the bow tie until later. Slipping on his socks, he picked up his shoes without even inspecting their shine, and walked back into the sitting room. Alex was still talking to Carys.

He hung back for a moment, just listening. Alex was articulating all of the feelings that Carys had told Leo about, letting her know that she wasn't alone. Just the right balance of understanding and hope. Somehow it touched him, in a way that he'd felt nothing could ever touch him again.

'I'm worried about my dad. He was driving, and we had an accident.'

Alex's face was fixed in an expression of intense concentration; she was staring at the phone. 'And how do you feel about that?'

'I keep telling him it's okay and it wasn't his fault, but he doesn't listen. Last night I heard him and Mum arguing again, and he was crying.'

Leo almost choked. Carys hadn't told him that, and if she had he wouldn't have known what to say. Because last night, sweating hard in the gym, he'd found tears in his eyes, thinking about all the *what ifs* that Alex had told him he shouldn't think about. He walked silently over to his seat by the window and sat down.

'Carys, it's really good that you're talking about this. Does your dad talk to anyone?'

'I don't think so. He and Mum are divorced.'

'Okay. I'm going to suggest something, and I want you to tell me if you think I'm on the right track. You've got a lot to cope with at the moment, and you can't help your dad as well. But there are lots of people who can. We have a families group, and they're really friendly. Might he come to something like that?'

'No, I don't think so. He says that he's okay, and that I'm the only one who matters now.'

'Well, I disagree. I think that both you and your dad matter, a very great deal.' Alex shot Leo a glance. Just one moment, but it seared through him, as if she were talking to him, not Carys.

'I asked him if he'd bring me to one of your meetings, the ones you were talking about on the radio yesterday…'

'And how does he feel about that?'

'He said it sounded like a great idea. But… I don't know if I can do all the things that you do…'

Alex chuckled. 'The whole point of it is that it doesn't matter what you can or can't do. We'd love you to come and just watch, maybe meet a few people. Some of us might be able to do a bit more than you, and some not so much, but it's all about valuing each other for who we are.'

'I'd like that.'

Carys's voice was steadier now, her manner more self-assured. Alex had given her something that Leo couldn't, a practical way forward, and the courage to take it.

'Okay, well, why don't you think about it, and I'll call you tomorrow. We can talk about what you want to do a bit more then, if you like.'

'I can't always talk… My mum doesn't know I'm call-ing…'

'In that case, do you want to text me? Whenever you like. I'll call you back.' Alex took her phone from her pocket. 'I'll text you now, so you've got my number.'

'Yeah. Thanks.'

Carys recited her number and Alex sent the text.

'Okay, I've got it. Will Leo be there? At the race meet-ing?'

'The one on Saturday? I think so.' She looked up at Leo and he nodded in confirmation.

'Is he as good-looking as he is on TV?'

Carys apparently thought that, since he'd said nothing for a while, he wasn't there, and Alex grinned suddenly, holding up one finger to silence him.

'I wouldn't like to say. You'll have to tell me what you think.'

Was that a giggle on the other end of the line?

'He's nice to talk to. I'll text you tomorrow, yeah?'

'Yeah. I'll be waiting to hear from you.'

They said their goodbyes, and Leo slumped back in his seat. Alex was smiling.

'What? Don't look so crestfallen; she said you were handsome.'

'Right.' Leo wondered whether Alex agreed with the assessment, and wished he had the nerve to ask her. 'Reduced to a piece of eye candy while you do all the meaningful work.'

'I'm not proud. If I need eye candy to get to speak to someone, I'll take whatever opportunities I can get.'

'Ah. And you call *me* a cynic.' Leo couldn't help smiling. It was Alex all over, not caring how she got her opportunities, but grabbing them with both hands.

'No, I think you called yourself a cynic. And I think it was a very nice compliment. Carys obviously felt at ease with you, and that helped her talk about the things which mattered to her. You have a problem with that?'

'No, no problem at all.' He bent down to slip on his shoes and tie the laces. She was flushed with success and so, so beautiful. Perhaps...

Leo wondered how long it would be before he stopped hesitating over asking the simplest, most innocent things. Persuading himself not to overthink them might be a good start. 'I don't suppose you'd like to come along tonight? There are going to be some interesting people there.'

If she'd just stop blushing every time, it would make asking easier. 'I don't think I'm dressed for it.'

Alex would outshine every woman in the room, whatever she was wearing. But he had to admit that she might *feel* a little out of place in jeans.

'Telling you that you'd make the whole room look overdressed isn't going to work, is it?' Leo took refuge in the charm that everyone expected from him, which Alex clearly didn't take all that seriously.

'No. That's a bit over the top for my liking.'

'We could swing past your place and you could slip into something suitable…' He laughed as she pulled a face.

'I'm not slipping into anything. Apart from my pyjamas.'

'Okay.' He wasn't sure whether it was a relief that she'd turned him down, or a disappointment. 'Don't suppose you're any good with a bow tie, are you?'

'Why? Surely you've got the hang of that by now.'

'It's my policy never to tie my own bow tie when there's a lady present.'

She rolled her eyes. 'Sounds a bit risky to me. What happens if they want to strangle you with it?'

Leo hadn't really expected Alex to fall for that one either, but it was becoming increasingly compelling to watch her not falling for his charm. He walked back into the bedroom, smiling.

Ever resourceful, Leo seemed to have solved the problem of whether or not he was going to watch her up the drive outside her block of flats. Instead of stopping on the road, he turned in and brought the car to a halt a dozen feet from the main door.

'I'll see you tomorrow afternoon, then?'

'You're coming?' She'd given Leo a copy of her calendar for the next month, but Alex hadn't thought he'd bother with an after-school session.

'If you don't mind. I'd like to see some of the training that goes into the event days.'

'You'll be very welcome. But I have to warn you that it's unlikely we'll get much of an audience. That kind of thing has very low ratings…'

He narrowed his eyes momentarily, then brushed the dig off. 'I'll survive. I might be a little bit late, depending on whether my surgery runs to time or not.'

'Right then. See you tomorrow. At whatever time you get there.'

She got out of the car and Leo turned in the driver's seat. He looked stunningly dapper in his dark suit and bow tie and now that Alex knew exactly what lay beneath his white dress shirt, there was an edge of hard craving to go with it. She almost wished that she could have said yes to tonight.

There was a small problem, though. Leo seemed to assume that she could just pop home and shimmy into a little black dress, but she didn't have anything that even approached that in her wardrobe. And, more to the point, she hadn't quite found that place where she could turn up at a social event on Leo's arm without feeling that made them more than friends. The *interesting people* would have to wait until she was more sure of herself.

The thought made her close the car door behind her with rather more vigour than she'd intended. Alex bent down, pulling her face into a foolish grin, and gave him a little shrug, as if she hadn't banked on her own strength. He waved her away from the car and when she stepped back it slid away.

'So. What's he like, then?' Rhona was busy taking off layers of clothing, to reveal a bright, ebulliently patterned dress. The heating engineers had been in first thing this morning and the radiators were pumping out heat, to the point that the windows had started to steam up.

'He's…complicated.'

If Alex had thought about her answer for more than five seconds, she would have known it would be like a red rag to a bull. Rhona pounced on the word.

'Good-looking and complicated. Sounds like the answer to a maiden's prayer.'

'Says the woman who's engaged to the most uncomplicated guy I've ever met.' Tom was solid, dependable and clearly just as head over heels in love as Rhona was.

'I didn't say that *complicated* made him a keeper. Where's my mug?'

'Here…' Alex reached into her drawer and held it out. 'Sorry. I tidied up a bit.'

'I thought the place looked a bit stark.' Rhona's idea of tidy was being able to see over the top of the piles of files, magazines and paperwork on her desk. But it was organised chaos and she could pull exactly the right thing from the pile at exactly the right time.

'You should see his flat. The only thing out of place in it was me.'

'You went to his flat?' Rhona grabbed her mug and sat down at her desk, clutching it. 'Do tell. Is he really a blond?'

'Of course he is. He was blond when I met him the first time.'

'So you got close enough to look at his roots, then?' Rhona grinned.

'I don't need to look at his roots; I know a natural blond when I see one. Just take my word for it.'

'Okay.' Rhona leaned back in her chair. 'Natural blond, *very* handsome, complicated. Tidy flat…although I don't necessarily hold that against him. Anything else?'

'Very good at what he does.'

'Aha! So you like him, then.'

'He's…got a lot of charm. And he's tall.' Alex decided to leave the bit about the great body out. Rhona was going to want a full description, and she'd been trying to forget all about what Leo might, or might not, have been doing with his great body last night. This morning's papers had pictures of a very famous, very beautiful woman walking down the steps of a smart-looking building. Holding tight to the arm that Leo had offered Alex last night.

'And… Come on, Alex, you always go for the serious

guys. Ever thought of a quick dalliance with someone who'll leave you with a smile on your face?'

'Leave me? You're seriously suggesting I go out with someone who I know is going to leave me?'

'Yeah. Don't knock it. He crashes in, rocks everyone's world and then leaves again. Five minutes of feeling good and then he doesn't look back. You need to waste your time with a few like him, before you can work out who the right guy is.' Rhona's thumb gravitated to the band of her engagement ring in the way it always did when she talked about the *'right guy'*.

Alex sighed. Leo was already rocking her world, and the experience wasn't altogether positive. He was charming, unpredictable, those flashes of commitment and compassion just enough to keep her wondering. Just enough to make her believe that there was more to him than met the eye, and that maybe he just needed someone to bring that out in him.

'I don't want someone who'll leave me. And I can't just tap him on the nose with my magic wand and get him to change. What's the first rule in the book? You think you can change them, but you can't.'

'True enough. So ten minutes of magic is out, then. I bet he'd make it interesting…'

Alex *knew* he'd make it interesting. And she'd thought about it—who wouldn't? But if the last ten years had taught her anything, it was to focus on the goals that were possible, not the ones which weren't.

'There's no point in wasting your energy going after things you can't have.'

'Your famous single-mindedness?' Rhona grinned. 'You *can* take some time out from that, you know.'

'What for? Life's beautiful. Why fill it with the things you know aren't going to work out?'

Rhona thought for a minute. 'Dunno. You've got me there. Want some coffee?'

'Yes, thanks. And thanks for the chat, Rhona...'

Rhona rolled her eyes but said nothing. There was nothing *to* say. It was all very clear in Alex's mind. Leo was handsome, complicated and wouldn't know what to do with a relationship if it smacked him in the face. And he wasn't the one she wanted.

CHAPTER SIX

BY THAT AFTERNOON the picture in the paper—the one Alex was ignoring because it was none of her business—had done its work. Nudging at the jealousy centres in her brain. Telling her that all the good she thought she saw in him was just her imagination, and stamping on any notion she had of trusting Leo any further than she could throw him.

It had taken her three months to get a permit for the teachers' car park, but when she arrived Leo's car was parked in one of the spaces reserved for the Year Heads. When she inspected the windscreen, there was a note on the school's headed notepaper giving him temporary permission to park there and when she shouldered her bag and walked towards the gym she saw Leo, wearing a fur-hooded parka, standing on the frozen ground by the entrance, talking to the headmistress.

Typical. Was there no one on the planet who was immune to Leo's charm?

'And Together Our Way provided training for your staff...?'

'Yes, we have a two-day workshop every summer, in the holidays. The first one was just for our staff, but last year we invited PE staff from schools all over the borough.' Belinda Chalmers was justifiably proud of the initiative her school had taken.

'And has this impacted the culture of sport in the school?

As a whole?' Leo was absorbed in the conversation and hadn't noticed Alex standing behind him.

'Have you ever seen the winners of a race turn round to cheer the losers on to the finish line? I hadn't, before I went to one of Alex's race meetings, but now the idea's caught on and it's something a lot of our children do.'

'Impressive. So the kids with disabilities aren't just struggling to keep up. They've been leading the way.' As usual, Leo's questions had led him to the very heart of the matter.

'Exactly.'

'And you take children from all over the borough? Not just this school?'

'Yes. But we don't have enough places for all of the children who want to come. Even though we have a new gym building, we only have so much space and equipment. And there's a very high ratio of trainers to children during the sessions, so we're limited by that as well.'

'I wonder… Do you think I might do a telephone interview with you for my show? It would be great to get someone who understands the wider impact of the work that Alex and her charity are doing.'

'Of course. I'd be very happy to talk about it.'

'Fabulous. I'll give you a call tomorrow if I may, and we can set something up.' Now that he'd finished with the questions, he finally noticed Alex's presence and his face broke into a broad grin. 'Hey. I've just been hearing…'

He broke off as a minibus edged its way into the space next to his car, brushing one of the wing mirrors so that it snapped forward. Alex heard Belinda Chalmers' sharp intake of breath.

'Oh, really. There's plenty of space on the other side…'

'Looks as if he's missed me.' Leo tried to divert her, but Belinda Chalmers was already marching across towards the car park, no doubt intent on giving the driver a piece of her mind.

'All the same. Your car's blocking the side door of the minibus, and it's easier for the children to get off that way. You might not be so lucky when he realises that and tries to back up again.' Alex squinted at the gap between the minibus and Leo's car.

'Yeah. You've got a point...' Leo pulled his car keys from his pocket and turned to stride towards the car park.

It seemed that the minibus driver had the same idea. He moved back a couple of inches then thought better of it and switched the engine off. Then the back doors of the minibus opened, and he jumped out and began to unload sports bags. There seemed to be some jostling going on inside the minibus and Leo suddenly increased his pace from a brisk walk into a run.

A boy jumped down from the back of the minibus while the driver's back was turned. 'Sit down everyone...' The driver's instruction came too late and another boy tumbled out after the first.

A high scream floated through the cold air. Then another. Alex dropped her bag and started to run towards the bus. She could see Leo kneeling beside the fallen child, who seemed to be fighting him off, and Belinda Chalmers climbing into the back of the minibus to restore order amongst the children who were still inside.

'Andrew... Andrew.' The boy who had fallen was almost hysterical and Alex knelt down beside Leo, trying to calm him.

'Get off me...' Andrew pulled himself up to a sitting position and aimed a punch at Leo's face. Apart from a sharp intake of breath, Leo didn't react.

'Andrew.' Leo took his cue from Alex and used the boy's name. He couldn't possibly know what the problem was, but he seemed to sense that there was one and held his hands up in a gesture of surrender. 'Listen... Listen. I'm not going to hurt you. I just want to make sure you're all right.'

He sat back on his heels, still holding his palms forward for Andrew to see. The boy stilled, staring at him intently.

'Not too keen on doctors, eh?' Leo smiled at him.

That was the understatement of the year. When Andrew had first come to the training sessions, he'd insisted that the doctors had stolen his left foot, and he hated them for it. He was working through that with his own doctors, who were slowly gaining his trust, but an unexpected injury and an unknown doctor were too much for him.

'Andrew, this doctor's like your doctor at the hospital, Dr Khan...' Alex shot Leo a glance, wondering if he'd play along, and he nodded. 'He's not going to touch you unless you tell him that he can.'

A rush of tears spilled suddenly down Andrew's cheeks. From the way he was holding his right leg, it looked as if he'd injured it when he fell, and it must be starting to hurt now. And the boy was reacting to the pain, trying to protect himself in the only way he knew how.

'Tell him... I don't want him.'

'Tell me yourself.' Leo's voice was gentle, seeming to understand everything. 'Loud and clear. Make sure I hear you...'

'I don't want you!' Andrew turned his head, shouting the words straight at Leo.

'Okay, that's fair enough. But will you let me just watch? I won't come any closer.'

Venting his feelings at the top of his voice seemed to have calmed Andrew, and he nodded silently. Leo slowly started to take his parka off and Alex caught the significance of the gesture. Taking it from him and laying it down on the icy ground, she sat down on it.

'You must be cold. Come here, eh?' Andrew let her lift him gently onto the warm down of Leo's jacket and she put her arm around him, hugging him close as the shivers of cold and fear subsided.

'That better?' Leo ventured a question.

Andrew nodded in reply, and Leo tried another. 'If you've hurt yourself...' He shrugged as if it wasn't completely obvious that Andrew had hurt his ankle. 'You could just point, if you felt like it. Perhaps let Alex take a little look?'

Andrew pointed at his ankle and Alex reached for his leg, pulling the soft fabric of his tracksuit bottoms up a little. The boy nestled against her without protest and she carefully took his trainer off and then his sock. The ankle was red and already beginning to swell, and Andrew looked at it mournfully. Injuring one of your 'good' limbs was every amputee's worst nightmare.

Leo's brow darkened, just for a moment. He'd know as well as Alex did that the ankle needed attention, but quite how they were going to do it without distressing Andrew even more was another matter.

'That doesn't look too bad to me. If we put a little bit of ice on it and a bandage it'll be better in no time.' Leo was deliberately looking on the bright side and assuming that there was no fracture, but it was the right thing to say. Andrew brightened visibly.

'We're in the way here, though.' Leo glanced up at the minibus, where Belinda Chalmers and two other teachers were keeping the children inside quiet and in their seats. 'Would you like to sit in my car?'

Andrew's gaze followed Leo's pointing finger. Whether by chance or design, Leo had picked the right thing. Andrew loved cars and his face lit up when he saw Leo's.

'I'm not sure how I'm going to get out of that parking spot. You want to come and give the hands-free parking a shot with me?'

Andrew nodded, and Leo bent forward slowly. The boy let him pick him up and carry him over to the passenger door of the car.

Alex followed him, brushing the dirt off his parka, and she reached into the pocket and found his car keys, unlocking the doors. Leo got in carefully, with Andrew still in his arms, sliding over into the driver's seat before depositing Andrew back in the front passenger seat.

'All right. We'll just buckle you up.' He pulled the seat belt across the boy, taking the opportunity to surreptitiously check on his ankle in the process. Then he closed the car door.

'Smooth operator.' Belinda Chalmers had got out of the minibus and stood next to Alex, watching as the car slid slowly out of its parking space, Andrew staring open-mouthed as Leo rather ostentatiously took his hands off the steering wheel.

Alex had been trying not to think about just how smooth. The charm that had convinced Andrew to accept his help was exactly the same as the charm which got him up to goodness knew what after dark.

'Has someone telephoned Andrew's mother? It looks like a sprain, but there's the possibility it may be a fracture.'

'She's on her way. I'll get the other children inside if you want to stay here.'

'Yes. Thanks.' Now that the side door of the minibus could be slid open, Alex would rather get the children into the gym and start the training session. Leo didn't appear to need her any more.

But there were three sports teachers, all qualified to supervise that, and Andrew was hurt and her responsibility until his mother got here. Her issues with Leo were completely incidental right now. Alex opened the door of Leo's car and slid into the back seat.

'How are you doing, Andrew?'

'Fine.' The boy was engrossed with the dashboard, and it was Leo who turned and grinned at her.

'What about letting Alex take a look at your ankle now, eh, Andrew? Must be hurting a bit.' Leo caught Andrew's hand, guiding it away from the control for the fog lamps just before he managed to switch them on.

'You can, if you want.' Andrew innocently chose Leo over Alex. Why not? Everyone else seemed to fall for his charm.

'Okay then. Thanks.' Leo leaned over, inspecting the ankle carefully, watching Andrew's face for any signs of pain as he gently rotated it. 'Well, that doesn't look too bad. Few days' rest and you'll be right as rain. I've got something to put on it to make it a bit more comfortable, though. Just until your mum gets here to take you home.'

Leo was saying all the right things. Reassuring Andrew that he wasn't badly hurt and that he'd be going home. The boy nodded and Leo got out of the car, bumping around in the boot.

'Want to see how this works?' He'd had the sense to just bring what he needed, not letting Andrew see his medical bag. Andrew nodded, and Leo bent his own hand, putting it inside the inflatable ankle splint.

By the time Andrew's mother hurried towards them, accompanied by Belinda Chalmers, Leo had coaxed Andrew into allowing him to put the splint around his ankle. He got out of the car, motioning for Andrew's mother to take his place in the driver's seat.

'Andrew... Are you all right?'

'Yes. Are we going home, Mum?'

'Let me speak to the doctor first...' Marion looked uncertainly up at Leo. She must have been told that Andrew was with a doctor, and was clearly surprised at how relaxed her son was with him.

'*No!* We're going *home*!' Andrew's face reddened.

Marion's face contorted into an expression of helplessness. 'Andrew...wait just a minute...please, love...'

'Hey, there.' Leo stepped in again. Always there, always charming everyone into doing exactly what he wanted them to. Alex was beginning to tire of watching it. 'Give me a minute to talk to your mum, eh? It's okay, we're not going to do anything you don't want to.'

He waited for Andrew's nod and then turned to Marion. 'It looks like it's just a sprain. But I'd like to get it X-rayed, just in case.'

Marion's face took on a pinched look. Clearly she wasn't looking forward to waiting with Andrew at the hospital, but she knew that it would have to be done. 'Yes. Thank you.'

'My surgery has a walk-in centre next door, and we make use of it for our patients. We can take him there, get him seen straight away and then I'll bring you back here.'

Marion pressed her lips together. 'That must be a private clinic. We don't have any insurance...'

'It won't cost anything. We have an arrangement with them.'

'Are you sure?' Marion looked uncertainly at Alex.

'If that's okay with Leo, then I think that would be better for Andrew.' It was a good offer, and Marion should take it.

'I really appreciate it. Thank you, doctor.'

'Call me Leo.' He cut through Marion's flustered gratitude and turned to Andrew. 'Right then. Here's the deal...'

She wanted desperately to go with them, just to be there for Andrew and Marion whether they needed her or not. But it appeared that Leo was the only person that either Andrew or his mother needed.

Alex climbed out of the car, walking back to where she'd dropped her sports bag. The training session had already started and, although she'd organised this evening so that she'd be free to show Leo around, she might as well go along anyway. At least she wouldn't have to deal with having to watch the Leo effect.

Leo had reckoned that Marion would like some time to talk alone with Andrew and he'd left them in his car together. Alex had got out of the car without so much as a word to say where she was going.

This evening she was different. She'd done all the right things, said all the right things, but the change was as

marked as if the sun had suddenly gone behind a cloud.
He wanted to know why. He didn't have time right now to
examine why he wanted to know; he just did.

'Aren't you coming with us?' He caught her up at the
door of the sports hall.

'You don't need me.'

He was tempted to tell her that he *did* need her, quite
desperately. That worked with most people, without any
need to elaborate on exactly why. But Alex was different
from most people and he wouldn't get away with it.

'Don't you want to come?'

She turned, and he caught a glimpse of scorn in her
eyes. Not quite the emotion he wanted, but then any emotion was generally better than none.

'Of course I do. But I should stay here and help with
the training...'

She still had a bit to learn about being in charge. 'You're
the Chief Executive of the charity, right?'

'I wouldn't put it quite like that. Sounds a bit stuffy...'

'You're the one who makes things happen, which makes
you a Chief Executive, whether you like it or not. Which
makes you responsible for leading the way, showing what
your core values are.'

She stared at him for a moment and then the penny
dropped. 'And one of our core values is that we never leave
anyone behind...' Suddenly she thrust her bag into his arms
and pushed open the door of the sports hall. 'Wait for me.
I'm just going to tell everyone that Andrew's okay but that
I'm going with him for his X-ray.'

As they walked behind Leo into the smart reception area
Marion caught Alex's arm, whispering to her, 'This place
looks very posh... We don't have health insurance—are
you sure it's free?'

'Don't worry. It's okay.' It didn't look free to Alex either. But this was the part of Leo that she could trust.

He was carrying Andrew upright, rather than cradled like a sack of potatoes. Probably not quite as comfortable for the boy's ankle, but it was protected by the splint and it changed the dynamic. Andrew wasn't helpless in his arms; he could lean across the reception desk and see what was going on, and the receptionist responded by smiling and talking to him.

She filled out a form and held it out for Andrew to take. He grabbed it and Leo nodded to her, smiling. 'I can take him straight through?'

'Yes, room nine.' The woman gave Leo a brilliant smile, which was over and above the requirements of her job, and undoubtedly just for him.

There was a brief interlude when Leo pretended to lose his way in the quiet, carpeted corridor, but Andrew put him right, pointing to the correct door. Inside, he waved Marion and Alex towards a couple of chairs and sat Andrew down on the examination couch, keeping the curtains that surrounded it open so that he could see his mother.

A woman in a brightly coloured top came in with a cup of tea for Marion and she took it awkwardly, still obviously worried about the cost of all this. Leo grinned at her. 'My surgery's just next door. We have an arrangement to use the clinic's facilities.'

'It's so good of you. The hospital's been wonderful with Andrew, but his usual doctor won't be there at the moment and the Urgent Care Centre...'

Leo nodded. 'I know. They do a great job, but sometimes you have to wait a bit. This is a lot easier for him.'

'Yeah.' Marion nodded.

It was a great deal easier. Andrew hardly seemed to notice Leo's gentle and thorough examination, nor did he protest when he was left alone for the X-rays to be taken.

'Looks fine to me…' Leo had reviewed the X-rays and confirmed that there was no fracture. 'I'm going to give you a support for your ankle, and I'd like you to wear it for a week or two until your ankle's strong again. But after that you'll be as right as rain. So I expect to see you at the training session in a couple of weeks, when I visit.'

'Can I ring you up when you're on the radio?' Andrew seemed to have given up on the question about going home now that it seemed likely he was just about to do so.

'Yes, if you want to. You have to have your mum do it, though. What do you want to talk about?'

'Your car.'

'Nah, no one's interested in that. What about your training sessions with Alex?'

'Maybe.'

Marion nodded. 'We'll call. I listened to the programme on Monday when we heard that Alex was going to be on.'

Leo turned. 'What did you think?'

'I thought it was great. It's really good that you're giving this some airtime. I wish we'd known sooner; I could have told more of my friends about it.'

Alex quirked her lips downwards. 'It was all a bit last-minute. We weren't the first choice.'

His gaze found hers, and suddenly it seemed as if he was talking only to her. The way he spoke to his listeners, as if each one was the only one. 'Alex stood in for us when someone else let us down. She's made everyone realise that we made a big mistake in not asking her first.'

She tore her gaze away from his, refusing to believe what he'd just said. It was just Leo making the best of things.

'I think you're being nice…' And she didn't particularly want him to be nice. She wanted the businesslike Leo who didn't tear at her heart whenever he turned his blue eyes onto her.

'I'm *never* nice.' He picked Andrew up, switching his attention back onto the boy. 'Come on then. Time to go home.'

He'd been able to do little enough for Andrew, simply called in a few favours to make things easier for him. But when they'd got back to the school, and the boy had given him a high five before his mother took him off home, it had warmed Leo. It was sometimes the little things that were the most rewarding.

'Thank you.' He was alone with Alex now, walking towards the car park after managing to catch the last ten minutes of the training session.

'You're welcome. Must be very difficult when the kids get hurt like that. They've already had a lot of trauma to contend with.'

'Yeah. Some of them take it in their stride, but others… Sometimes the ones you need to watch the most are the ones who just go quiet.'

'That's my experience too.' He wondered whether he should mention that Alex seemed to have *gone quiet* on him, but wasn't sure where to start.

He decided to try an experiment. 'Did you see the report in the papers this morning?'

'No.'

Gotcha. Her voice was bristling with discomfort, and she hadn't even asked what report. Leo stopped to face her and she pretended not to notice and kept on walking.

'Fast-track,' he called after her and she turned slowly.

'What?'

'Fast-track. I ask you to come along to a drinks party, you say no and then I'm in the paper, leaving with Evangeline Perry…'

'So what? You can walk down a set of steps with someone, can't you? I do it all the time.' She pressed her lips together, knowing she'd given herself away fully now.

'I had my arm around her. That was because half a dozen

paparazzi had suddenly appeared out of nowhere and were in her face.' Leo usually left the press to come to whatever conclusions they liked, preferring to just rise above it all and get on with his job. But this time it mattered to him.

'What you do is none of my business, Leo.'

'No, I know it isn't. But, despite that, I have an irrepressible urge to explain that I've known Evie for years, and she and I were just talking about some of the issues that you and I have been covering on my show…'

'Oh, pull the other one, Leo…' At last, an honest response. This, he could work with.

'Evie's sister used to run for the American national team. She contracted meningitis last year and that's put a stop to her career for the time being. Arielle always said that she wanted to work with kids when she took a step back from competing, and this project's been bubbling under for a while now…'

'And you just happened to bump into her sister at this drinks do.'

'No, I'd arranged to see Evie there—that was one of the reasons I asked you to come. She was there with her partner—he's the guy behind us on the steps.' He paused for a moment to see whether Alex was going to come up with something in reply, but she just stared at him dumbly.

'Of course she lent a bit of much-needed glamour to what was otherwise quite a dry evening. But that was incidental…'

What was he saying? The one thing that never went down well with women was calling another woman glamorous. They wanted to know that they were the only person in the room.

'Is she the same in real life?'

'She's a nice person.'

'I meant is she as beautiful? I saw her last film…'

'Evangeline's a film star. It's her job to be beautiful.

She doesn't get paid for being nice, but she's that too. She's promised to give me an interview for the show on Friday.'

'Right. Good.' Alex seemed lost for words, wrenching open the door of her car and throwing her sports bag onto the back seat.

'Are you going to listen in?'

'I'll try.' She got into the car and the engine growled into life. Then Alex reversed out of her parking space so quickly that she almost shunted into the back of his car. Leo grinned. She'd be listening.

CHAPTER SEVEN

LEO THE IMPOSSIBLE. Being with him was like standing in a hall of mirrors, unable to tell whether the man in front of her was the real Leo or just a reflection.

She guessed from the smug look that Leo had given her as she drove off that he knew she'd be listening on Friday, but she did it all the same. Evangeline spoke passionately about her sister's illness and how it had prompted them both to think about setting up a scheme for young athletes with disabilities. Alex was sorry she'd misjudged her. But she knew she hadn't misjudged Leo. Whether he was lost to her because of another woman or because he was a different person now didn't really matter. He was lost to her and that was it.

If she'd remembered that, it would have made life a good bit easier. But instead she'd been jealous of Evangeline and, worst of all, Leo knew that now. Monday was going to be difficult.

She arrived at the radio station early. She'd thought about this and if there was going to be an atmosphere between her and Leo the listeners would know it. She had to clear the air. Half an hour alone in the restroom preparing herself only made her more nervous, and then Leo breezed in.

'Ready to go?' He smiled at her.

'Leo… Leo, wait.' Better get it over with now. 'I'm sorry. About the picture in the paper and…'

He turned his bright blue eyes on her and she fell silent, feeling her cheeks flush.

'The paparazzi jumped to the same conclusion and so did everyone who read the paper. Why not you?'

'It was none of my business.'

'I put myself out there, Alex. I have to accept that what I do is sometimes noticed. I care about what you think, which is why I bothered to explain myself.'

That… That sounded suspiciously like a compliment. 'Are you being nice?'

His smile. That luminous look which seemed to hide no secrets. 'Nah. I'm never nice.' He looked at his watch. 'We've got to get going now. Do you have ten minutes afterwards? I just need to discuss a few details for next week.'

When they got into the studio, it all clicked. He smiled. She smiled. She managed to find answers for the callers' questions. She saw what nerves had obliterated last Monday—that Leo was feeding her all the time, never making statements, always leaving what he said open for discussion. The hour flew.

Justin was smiling when he walked into the studio, after they'd handed over to the next presenter. 'Fabulous. Both of you.'

Leo seemed suddenly a little off-key. 'Yeah, I enjoyed it.'

'Follow-ups?' Justin held up a manila envelope and Leo gestured in Alex's direction.

'Alex might like to take those.'

'Yes. Thanks.'

'There was something else…' Leo was on his feet before Justin could get the rest of the sentence out.

'Yeah. That's in hand, Justin. Is the car waiting?'

'No, it's not here yet. As we've got a few minutes…'

'Later.' The one word was so final that even Justin got

the hint. Leo picked up Alex's coat, holding it out in an unequivocal intimation that she should put it on. Then he practically frogmarched her out of the studio.

'What's this all about, Leo?' This was one version of Leo that she hadn't seen in the hall of mirrors yet.

'Can we talk in the car?' He caught the attention of the show's production assistant, who was passing in the corridor. 'Jo, have you called the car yet?'

'No, Justin said to wait…'

'Yeah, I expect he did. Could you do me a favour and give them a call now?'

This was crazy. Leo obviously had something he wanted to say privately, and it seemed to be bothering him. So much so that he was prepared to spend almost an hour driving needlessly around London.

She tugged at his sleeve. 'I could do with some coffee first…'

He shot her a smile. 'In that case… Jo, forget about the car. I'll call them.'

'Sure thing, Leo…' Jo broke off and watched as Leo hustled her away.

It was beginning to snow outside, large flakes drifting past streetlights and car headlamps. Almost a picture book scene. Leo offered his arm and Alex took it, her gloved hand resting lightly on the inside of his elbow.

This was ridiculous. He talked about all kinds of intimate issues to all kinds of people for a good proportion of his time. Putting things clearly and without embarrassment was part of his job, and he was good at it.

They walked in silence for a few moments and then she held her free hand out, catching snowflakes in her palm. 'First snow of the winter.'

'Yeah.'

'I like it when it's like this. Fresh and clean, ready for my footprints…'

'Me too.' It occurred to Leo that she was trying to put him at his ease. That thought was even more confusing because that was usually his job as well.

He opened the main door to his apartment block, standing aside to let her go first. Smiling to the security guard, he escorted her to the lift.

When he ushered her into the lounge, she gasped, walking over to the window. 'Oh, it's beautiful, Leo. Is it always like this when it snows?'

'Not always.' The sky seemed almost luminous, a pinkish-white bank of cloud hovering over London. Large flakes of snow drifted past the window and, further away, the falling snow gleamed on the rooftops. Maybe he'd just never noticed it before.

Leo walked over to stand next to her and she turned her shining face up towards his. 'I bet if you stood here on Christmas Eve you'd see Santa's sleigh up there somewhere.'

Maybe he would have, if Alex had been here. She was doing it again, trying to put him at his ease, but somehow that didn't matter quite so much now. He grinned down at her. 'I'll go and make the coffee.'

'The coffee was just an excuse. I don't really want it.'

In other words: *Just get on with it.* Leo couldn't have put it better himself.

'Justin wants us to talk about sex…' He grimaced. Surely there was a better way of putting it than that, but all the usual polish seemed to rub off when he was alone with Alex.

She raised her eyebrows. 'Really? I'd better take my coat off then.' She slipped off her padded jacket, draping it over the back of the sofa, and then turned to face him. 'Go on then. I'm all ears.'

She was teasing him, and it wasn't helping. Leo felt enough like a tongue-tied teenager already.

'All right. Make it easy, won't you.' He shot her a warning look. 'Justin's been very pleased with the way that you've covered a lot of the wider issues, and he's come up with this. I told him that I had my reservations and that I'd talk to you about it.'

She thought for a moment. 'I think it's a good idea. We cater for young people up to twenty-one and the physical side of relationships can be an issue for them. What are your reservations?'

'The first is that you've been speaking very candidly about your own experiences. And that's been great, but I don't want to put you in a position where you feel railroaded into sharing things you want to keep personal.'

She nodded. 'Okay. Well, I think I'd rather take that one as it comes. In principle, I'm happy to talk about anything if it's going to help someone.'

'Fair enough. But I want you to remember that we're on the radio. I have a personal objection to having any guest talk about things they're not comfortable with.'

'Thanks. I appreciate that. What's the other thing?' Her gaze caught his suddenly, tangling him in its web. Alex's eyes had the power to leave him shaking, babbling all kinds of nonsense, and Leo tried not to look at them.

'I think this is a fine line to walk. I don't want to minimise the practical difficulties that a disability can cause, because I've seen a lot of those kinds of issues amongst my own patients. But, at the same time, it would be wrong to imply that having a disability means you necessarily *have* to have a problem with physical intimacy.'

Her face broke into a brilliant smile. 'Since you know that without needing to be told, doesn't that make you the ideal person for me to try this out with?'

For one dizzy moment Leo thought that she meant *actually* try it out. Up close and deliciously personal.

'Why don't we do this?' She brought him back down from the furthest reaches of fantasy with a bump. 'We'll talk about the effects of losing a limb on body image. Then, if anything comes of that and a caller asks specific questions, we can answer them.'

That was probably the way that Leo should have put it in the first place, and the fact that he'd made a perfectly straightforward issue as embarrassing as possible wasn't lost on him. 'Yeah. That sounds good. As long as you're completely happy with that.'

She nodded, turning to him suddenly. 'I'm fine with it. And I really appreciate you asking. I think the only point I really want to get over is that someone who really cares about you will take you the way you are. And that communication's the key thing.'

'Which applies to all of us, I guess.'

'Yes. It does. Can we sit down now?'

She never would have believed it, but it was actually quite sweet. Leo, tongue-tied about sex. Yet another facet of the enigma which, despite all her efforts, became more pressing to solve every time she met him.

'What made you take up being a radio doctor?' She sat down on one of the large designer sofas and Leo sprawled opposite on its twin.

'I happen to think that being there for people is important. Many of the people who phone feel they've no one else to turn to. For three hours a week, I get to be the one that they can call.'

'And the rest of the time?'

There was a trace of sadness about his smile. 'I just have to hope that the time I have might make a difference somewhere. It's not an exact science.'

'When we first met… You so wanted to be on the cutting-edge, saving lives…'

'When we first met, I was dressed as a spaceship captain. I changed my mind about that as well.'

'You did look very dashing. Ready to fly off into the unknown and take over new worlds.'

He shook his head. 'That was more my brother's style. I was always the sensible one.'

'You didn't say you had a brother…'

'We were identical twins, and he still managed to be a lot better-looking than me. I kept him under wraps.'

'Were…?' There was something about the way he said it. 'May I ask?'

'I wish more people did.' Maybe it was a trick of the light, the luminous sky banding the carpet with reflections which merged into the subdued lighting in the room. But when he turned his blue eyes up towards her, Alex thought she saw the young man she'd first met looking at her.

She swallowed hard, trying to dislodge the lump in her throat. She knew how hard it was when people tried not to mention things that mattered.

'What was your brother's name?'

She thought she saw a smile flicker on his lips. 'Joel. He died six months after we first met. Just before Christmas.'

'I'm sorry. Really sorry, Leo.'

'Don't be. No one talks about him all that much and…' He shrugged. 'Sometimes I wish that everyone would just stop trying to spare my feelings.'

'I imagine they mean well.'

He nodded. 'Yes. I imagine that they do. But Joel should have more than just silence.'

'I'm happy to make some noise with you.'

Leo nodded. 'Sounds good to me. Join me in a brandy?'

'No, thanks.'

He walked over to a cabinet beneath the huge swirling picture on the wall, opening it and taking out a glass.

'Joel suffered from depression. He didn't tell anyone, but I knew something was up and confronted him. I persuaded him to go to the doctor, and when we found it was months before he could get to see a counsellor on the NHS we put what money we had together and he went privately to see someone.'

He turned, amber liquid swirling in the brandy glass in his hand. 'Not that it did any good. Joel took his own life.'

'But you tried. You were there for him…'

'Not when it mattered. And I should have told my parents—maybe they could have done something. Joel asked me not to.'

'Then you were respecting his wishes, weren't you?'

'Sometimes you have to act, despite what people ask you to do.' He took a sip from his glass and then another larger one, as if the first hadn't done anything to offset the pain. Alex doubted the second would either.

'And that's why you volunteered to work on the student helplines? For Joel?'

'Yeah. I wasn't there for him and the only thing that made me feel any better about that was being there for other people…' He took another sip of his drink, as if to stop some deathly cold creeping over him.

Suddenly the hall of mirrors came crashing down. The charming Leo, the businessman, the cynic and the doctor. All of his inconsistencies suddenly made sense.

Leo was exactly what he appeared to be. A passionate, dedicated man who had been broken by guilt and regret. The fame, the ratings on his radio show—they were just a way of reaching people. And he'd sworn himself to that— dedicating his energy to people he didn't know because people you didn't know couldn't hurt you.

'I know what you're thinking.' He spoke softly. 'It's been said often enough to me. I should let it go.'

'You're good but you're not a mind-reader, Leo.' A force that was nothing to do with her own will, and everything to do with the look in his eyes, impelled her to her feet and drew her across the room to where he stood.

'A lot of people aren't that hard to read…' His gaze searched her face.

'Go on then, if you think you can.'

He laid his index finger lightly on the side of her brow,

frowning as if some great mental effort was in progress. 'Huh…interesting. Very interesting.'

For a moment it was as if he *could* see what she was thinking. *Impossible. Snap out of it.*

'What's interesting?'

'I can't read you. I never quite know what you're going to do next. Fascinating.' The curve of his lips made it clear that was a compliment.

She knew that it was just Leo's charm, his way of turning a situation around and removing the barbs. But it was still compelling, and when she looked into his eyes she felt that he really did find her fascinating. Alex swallowed hard.

'You know what, Leo? Even if you could read minds, you still wouldn't be able to see into the future.'

'I think the universe has something to answer for there. We can see the past but it's too late to go back and do things differently. And the future…' He shrugged.

The one time frame that mattered the most was the one that Leo seemed unable to get to grips with. 'What about now, Leo?'

If she hadn't been so beautiful he could have shrugged *now* off. Leo could have forgotten her scent and dismissed the idea that he didn't have to reach very far in order to touch her.

'Now is…just a moment. Gone before you have a chance to even know what to do with it.'

She reached her hand out as if to catch snowflakes. Then she closed her fingers tight. 'There. Got it.'

Time really did seem to stand still, and it was the oddest feeling. One of complete warmth, absolute safety from a world that couldn't throw anything at him because it was suspended, waiting for Alex to allow it to start turning again.

'What will you do with it?' Alex turned her gaze onto him and Leo knew exactly what he wanted to do.

'I want to tell Tara that I'm sorry I didn't get to see her again. I want to tell *you* that I'm sorry…for everything. For not being there and…'

She laid one finger across his lips and it was all that Leo could do not to frame a kiss. 'I think *everything* pretty much covers it, Leo. If I tell you that you're forgiven, can we put that behind us? Where it belongs, in the past.'

Somehow that seemed possible. Anything seemed possible as long as it was contained in this one moment and couldn't spill out into their lives. He caught her hand, turning it in his to press a kiss against her palm.

Alex smiled. 'Captain Boone and Tara. Let them kiss goodnight and slip away into the universe? Leave us to get on with the things *we* have to do.'

Maybe she was right. Ten years ago he'd let the chance to kiss her slip away. He'd regretted it then and the thought of repeating that mistake now was unbearable.

'I'd like that.'

What harm could there be? If it could help Leo to let go, why not? One of the points of fancy dress was that you got to do things you might not normally do, and if anyone questioned them afterwards you could say you were just *in character*. Alex extended two fingers in a rough imitation of Tara's immobility gun, prodding her middle finger against the side of his ribs.

Leo grinned. 'So you've seen that episode, have you?'

The one where Tara held Captain Boone at gunpoint, then kissed him. She'd seen it. 'I watched an awful lot of TV when I was recovering from the accident.'

'And now you're putting it to good use…' He held out his hands, as if she really did have a gun on him. But his smile beckoned her. Grabbed her and dragged her in.

She brushed her lips against his.

'Nice. Very nice…' She felt his words form against her cheek and Alex drew back, teasing him for a moment.

Then she kissed him, trailing her lips from his mouth to the side of his jaw.

'Even nicer...' He kissed her fingers when she put her free hand to his lips, and then waited. He knew that she'd come back for more and when she did she made it a proper kiss, her hand wrapped around the back of his neck, her lips parted as they met his.

Leo let her draw away again, the broad smile on his face showing that he liked giving her the upper hand for a while, but they both knew it was never going to last. Alex kissed him again, feeling the softness of his lips, the strong brush of his jaw. She felt hard muscle flex and suddenly he gripped her wrist, pulling her arm up, her fingers away from his ribcage. His other arm pulled her against him and he turned her around, crowding her backwards against the wall.

Then *he* kissed *her*. Tender at first and then with a mounting hunger which made her gasp. Leo knew just how to kiss a woman. Enough control to let her know that he could produce almost any reaction he wanted, and yet just the right amount of surrender.

His lips left a trail of fire across her cheek. She felt his teeth gently nip at the lobe of her ear and she gasped. 'Tara...'

The retreat to the character's name was no mistake. This wasn't real, and he was telling her so. Just something they both wanted to do before their real lives reasserted themselves. He kissed her again, this time soft and slow. She knew there would be nothing more. There was a trace of regret in his eyes, as if he was finally waving Tara goodbye.

'I'm glad we waited.' His body was no longer pressing against hers, and he let go of her wrist. 'If I'd done that when I was twenty-one, it would have totally blown my mind.'

'And now?'

'It's totally blown my mind.' He chuckled, whirling her

around in a loose embrace and planting a kiss on her fore-head. 'But I'm not going to make any promises to call.'

'Because…?' She knew why. However much she ached for Leo, he wasn't the man she wanted.

'It's a while since I gave anyone my full attention.'

And he wouldn't give it to her. For a while maybe, it would seem so, but Leo always had something else on his agenda. He was afraid of missing anything. He'd committed himself to watching and waiting because he'd missed the most important moments of his life, the moments in which he could have answered Joel's calls.

'And I deserve nothing less.'

He grinned. 'Right in one. Can I get you something else? A drink maybe?'

He was doing this well. Making it clear that she was welcome to either stay or go, and that even if the kiss had been just one moment in time it wasn't one he regretted. And that was why she had to go.

'I should probably get home. Will you call the car for me, please?' She picked up his glass, imagining that she could taste his lips on the rim before the brandy hit her tongue.

He nodded and made the call. The car arrived within minutes and Leo escorted her downstairs, holding the door open for her and exchanging a quiet word with the driver, as if he'd just entrusted him with something precious. Then he watched as the car drew away.

Maybe she should text him, the way she'd done that morning, from the bus. She took her phone out of her bag, but that was as far as she got. That was something that had started a long time ago, but tonight had been the final ending.

CHAPTER EIGHT

LEO AS A FRIEND. A good-looking, charming friend who seemed to get just how she felt, and who might be around for longer than just a fleeting love affair. It was a thought. Stranger things had happened...

They could have lunch from time to time, talk about their lives and promise to see each other again some time soon. No pressure. No expectations. It wouldn't matter that Leo was so bound up with the past that he couldn't contemplate anything more than a slightly distant relationship with the present.

All of that assumed that Alex could forget about the kiss. It was just one kiss. How difficult could it be? Particularly when the need to think about Saturday's race meeting was so pressing.

The attendance of an outside broadcast crew had persuaded the manager of the sports centre they normally used to allow Together Our Way to take over the main track instead of being consigned to the cramped practice track. A lot was hanging on this and it *had* to go well.

There was still more than an hour to go before the start of the meeting but Alex saw his car in the car park outside the sports centre when she arrived. He was inside, fiddling with his phone, and when she rapped on the window he looked up.

His eyes. His smile...

Her skin began to tingle and Alex reminded herself yet again that she wasn't supposed to be thinking about the kiss. It had been an ending, not a beginning.

Leo finished typing a message on his phone and swung out of the car, reaching back inside to pull a bag from the back seat.

'You're joining in?' Or perhaps the sports bag was just for show.

'Thought I might just give the impression that I would, if asked.'

'Okay. What happens if I don't ask?'

'You'll ask.' He started to walk towards the sports centre and she fell into step beside him. 'You won't be able to resist putting me up against a bunch of skinny kids and watching them beat me.'

'You're thinking that you'll bravely suffer the humiliation of letting them win, are you?'

'I'm thinking that I'd be proud to run with them. And I respect them enough to give it my best shot. Are you running?'

'Yes. Think you can beat me?'

'I'll try…' His phone beeped and he pulled it out of his pocket. 'Ah. She's just arriving. I took the liberty of asking someone along, I hope you don't mind.'

'Of course not. But they're a bit early—it doesn't start for another hour.' Alex followed Leo's gaze to where a black SUV was manoeuvring into a parking space. 'Who is it—someone from the radio station?'

'Um…no.' He was looking suddenly awkward. 'I… Evie's sister's over from the States for a couple of weeks, and I asked them to come.'

'You did what? Evangeline Perry!' Alex looked over to the SUV, where a tall, slim woman was getting out of the passenger seat. Her hair was wound beneath a baseball cap and the peak obscured most of her face. 'You asked a film star to my race meeting? Leo, you might have mentioned it.'

'Why, so you could run around panicking? That's exactly why I didn't say anything about it. They're here because they're interested in what you're doing, and they'll keep a low profile.'

'Keep a low profile! Leo, didn't it occur to you that people might recognise her?'

'Of course it did. You said it would be good for the kids to have someone showing a bit of interest. And Evie's not high maintenance. Her minder will look after her.'

'Minder! For goodness' sake, Leo, if you're trying to disrupt things…' He'd lulled her into a false sense of security with his careful way of including her in every decision. 'I told you that you couldn't just swan in and take over. The kids are always the most important ones.'

'That's why Evie's here. Because the kids are important and she wants to show them some support. Give her the benefit of the doubt, will you…'

'I'm more than happy to give her the benefit of the doubt. You, I'm not so sure about.'

'Don't worry about sparing my feelings, will you.' He was grinning broadly, laughing as he turned to wave to the two women who were walking across the car park, followed by a man who sauntered behind them.

'Leo…' The woman in the baseball cap greeted him with a smile and they exchanged kisses. 'We made it.'

She turned to Alex, holding out her hand. 'Hi, I'm Evie Perry. You must be Alex.'

Close up, she was beautiful. Creamy skin, huge green eyes, with strands of Evangeline Perry's trademark red hair escaping her cap. Her jeans and warm jacket were casual but didn't look as if they came from the high street, and couldn't conceal her tall, willowy figure. If Evangeline Perry thought she needed to introduce herself then she was mistaken.

It was impossible not to feel somehow dowdy and lacking next to her, and that wouldn't have mattered so much if Leo hadn't been there. Alex took Evie's hand, trying not to tremble.

'Thank you so much for coming. I'm… I wish I'd known you'd be here—I could have…done something.'

Evie laughed. 'From what Leo said the other night, you're already doing a great deal. He couldn't stop talking about you.' She smiled at Leo and he winced, as if he'd been caught out doing something he shouldn't.

The thought that, in the presence of such a woman, Leo would have one thought in his head for her was… Well, it was something to think about. But Evie gave her no opportunity.

'This is my sister, Arielle. She's very interested in what you've achieved here and, as we're looking to set up a scheme something like this in the States, we're here to learn from you.'

'I… I'm sure there's not a lot I could teach you… But I'd love it if you'd come and meet some of the kids…'

'That's what we're here for.' Arielle's smile was just as warm as her sister's and Alex grinned back stupidly, not sure of what to say.

'Right, ladies.' Leo had picked up her sports bag along with his own and started to make for the entrance of the sports centre. 'No point in standing around here…'

For once, Leo's no-nonsense way of making things happen was a boon. Someone had recognised Evie on their way into the auditorium and word had gone round the small group of competitors and helpers who were already there, like a whispered shock wave. He gently made a path for Evie and Arielle down to the running track, and then pushed Alex forward to introduce them to the group that was beginning to crowd round.

She saw Hayley at the back of the group, her eyes shining. Alex leaned over, pulling her a little closer.

'This is Hayley—she's our best runner.'

'Not as good as you…' Hayley clasped Arielle's hand and didn't let go. Clearly she knew exactly who Arielle was.

'What distances do you run?' Arielle gave her a dazzling smile.

Hayley was too busy hero-worshipping and seemed to have forgotten. Alex prompted her.

'Hayley's best event is the thousand metres. But she's pretty good over shorter distances as well.'

'Ah, an all-rounder. So what's your best time over the thousand metres?'

'I… Not as good as yours.'

Arielle laughed. 'Well, I've been doing this a bit longer than you. Can I see?'

Hayley looked around wildly. Apparently she'd also forgotten the notebook she kept in her sports bag, noting all of her times, along with the dates.

'Hayley, go and get your book. Show Arielle your times.'

Hayley dropped Arielle's hand suddenly and pushed through the group to the side of the track. Arielle flashed Alex a smile and followed her.

The initial frenzied excitement at Evie and Arielle's arrival had subsided to an elated buzz. Rhona was dealing with the sound engineers and the seating area was beginning to fill up. The first competitors were beginning their warm-up routines and everything seemed to be working like a well-oiled machine. Alex had sat down by the side of the track, feeling suddenly surplus to requirements.

'Everything okay?' Leo sat down beside her.

She turned to him, smiling. 'Thank you. You were right, Leo.' He probably knew that already, but Alex wanted to be the first to say it.

He shrugged. 'Have you taken Evie's number?'

'No. Am I supposed to?'

He sighed. 'It would be good to think about these things. You're a good contact for her to make and she and Arielle can help you too.'

'That sounds a bit cold-blooded, doesn't it?'

'No, it's not at all. You both have the same priorities, don't you?'

'Yes, I suppose so. But it's so good of them to come; I can't ask any more of them.'

He rolled his eyes, taking his phone from his pocket. Alex averted her eyes. Probably a message from someone that Leo couldn't help but take. He typed for a moment and then her own mobile beeped.

'Done.' He put his phone away and Alex withdrew hers from her pocket. A text from Leo, to both her and Evie. She looked up towards the top of the stand, where Evie was sitting with a group of parents, and saw her turn, look at her phone and then wave down at them.

'Leo…' She felt herself flush awkwardly. Her phone beeped again and she looked at the text.

Making yourself useful, Leo? Please keep my number, Alex. Will call you.

'See…' Leo leaned in, looking over her shoulder.

Her whole body screamed at her to relax against him, and her mind told her to keep her distance. Good sense won out and she blanked the screen, feeling the pressure of his shoulder against hers relax.

'I'm not very good at this. Networking…' Leo seemed to do it all so effortlessly, knowing exactly the right thing to do in any given circumstance.

'No, you're not. You're good at making the magic. Leave the rest to us lesser mortals.'

Hard truth, laced with a compliment. Or maybe the other way round; it was impossible to tell with Leo. Somehow he managed to make it sound real, the two twisted together in a complex, sparkling spiral that sent shivers down her spine.

She should be doing something useful, not spending her time sitting here, however good it felt. 'Do you have an interview schedule or something? Anything I can help with?'

'I expect there is one. What I really need is a mike, though.' He signalled to one of the sound engineers who came hurrying over, putting a microphone in his hand.

'Thanks.'

'And here's the running order...'

'Okay.' He had the grace to deliver a sheepish grin as he stuffed the paper in his pocket without even looking at it.

'We'll start over there, with an introduction...'

'Yeah. Would you mind giving me a minute...?' Leo got to his feet, making in the opposite direction.

'Is he always like that?' Alex heard Rhona's voice behind her, and the sound engineer nodded.

'Yeah. We give him a list, he ignores it and we end up following him around, not sure what he's going to do next.'

'And that makes good radio?' Alex couldn't help but ask.

'Yeah. It makes great radio. That's why he gets away with murder, and no one ever complains.' The sound engineer shrugged, walking back over to his colleague.

'Going to go try keeping him under control, then? Just for the sake of appearances.' Rhona nodded at Leo's retreating back.

'Suppose so.' Alex got to her feet, walking over towards Leo.

Everyone had been persuaded to sit down, despite the air of excitement running around the auditorium. The place was packed, the usual parents and families joined by people who'd heard about the meeting from the radio. Leo handed Alex the microphone, showing her how to mute it, and when she spoke into it her voice sounded disconcertingly through the speakers that the sound engineers had set up.

'You do it…' She covered the microphone with her hand and feedback squealed through the speakers.

'Too busy.' He shot her his melting grin and left her to it. Alex took a deep breath and haltingly started to thank everyone for coming. A roar of applause greeted her mention of Evangeline and Arielle, and then another for Leo.

'And, on behalf of the young people who are competing today, I'd like to welcome you all. Please show them how much you're looking forward to this afternoon…' She was almost breathless, carried away by the noise and determined that the kids should have the biggest round of applause.

Evangeline and Arielle were both on their feet and Leo suddenly reappeared from whatever he'd been busy with, arms held above his head, clapping. Alex could almost feel the din of cheering and clapping vibrating through the air, and when she looked over towards the group of competitors waiting by the starting line their faces were shining.

They'd done it. Together, they'd made this moment. All the hard months of training, raising the money they'd needed, the teaching and the encouragement, had been down to her. But Leo had taken all that and given the kids something to remember.

She thrust the microphone back into his hand and hurried to her seat by the side of the track. Alex didn't want him to see that this thing, the huge, roaring wave of response that they'd created between them, had brought her close to tears. And she didn't want to think about all the other things that they might achieve together, because Leo wouldn't be here for long.

The races started. Personal bests were shattered as the crowd cheered all the competitors on. Alex kept herself busy by the track side, making sure that everyone was warmed up and ready for their races. It was a difficult line to walk, encouraging everyone to do their best but reminding them not to get carried away and injure themselves in the process, and she made sure that she spoke to each of the young athletes before their races.

Then the first interval. Leo was still at the side of the track, a group of competitors gathered around him. Little Sam, the boy whose photograph she'd thrust in front of him when they'd met at the hotel, was hovering on the edge of the crowd, watching silently.

He caught sight of him and leaned over towards him. 'What's your name...?' Leo bent down as everyone made way for Sam to get closer.

'Sam.'

'Hi, Sam. And what will you be doing today?'

Sam eyed him thoughtfully. Alex knew he was a child of few words and massive determination. 'Running.'

'Sounds good.' Leo rose to the challenge, clearly not about to give up just yet. 'And are you taking part in any of the events?'

'Yes.'

'Well, good luck. Let's hear a round of applause for Sam...'

Leo was working his way around everyone, and the spectators quickly got the idea of what was expected of them. Each child got a round of applause before Leo went on to the next.

'Thanks, Hayley.' He turned to the second of the two girls who stood clutching each other's hands, and Alice spoke up immediately.

'I'm Alice. I want to say something.' Alice's cheeks were flaming red but she had that determined look on her face that Alex had seen time and time again. Leo tipped the microphone towards her and she took it out of his hand, as if she was afraid she might not get to speak her piece.

'What is it you want to say, Alice?'

For a moment Alice wavered and Alex saw Hayley take

her hand, squeezing it. 'My leg was amputated two years ago...' The stadium had fallen silent suddenly, in response to the urgency in Alice's voice. She looked around wildly.

'And then what?' Leo's voice, gently encouraging her. Alice focused suddenly on his face and he nodded her on.

'I used to run for my county, and I'm training again now with the charity. I want to tell everyone that...' Alice dried up suddenly.

Alex started to push towards them. Alice didn't talk much about how desperately she wanted to run again, but somehow she'd screwed up the courage to share it with all these people. But this was enough. Good radio, good publicity for the charity, it all came second to Alice's best interests and she didn't want Leo pushing her.

He'd reached out, taking the microphone back and muting it. 'That's great, Alice. Is there something more you want to say?'

Alice nodded.

'Okay then, take a breath and just look at me. Forget about everyone else and say it to me. Whenever you're ready...'

'I'm ready.' Alice leaned towards him. 'I want to say that you can do more than you think. If you just try.'

A ripple of applause ran around the spectators, and Leo held his hand up for silence.

'That's something I could do with remembering...' Alex heard Leo's voice catch suddenly, as if he had something lodged in his throat. 'What do you do during your sessions at Together Our Way?'

'I can't run yet; I need a blade for that. But while I'm waiting I'm improving my fitness by exercising and I can jog... And I like the climbing wall.'

'I'll be looking for some advice on that, when I check it out next week.' Leo shot Alice a grin and she beamed back at him, flushed with her own achievement. 'Ladies and gents...'

He didn't even have to say it. The audience was his, and he knew it. One movement of his hand and they roared their approval, while Alice and Hayley clutched each other, waving to the crowd.

CHAPTER NINE

'ALEX!'

She looked round and saw Hayley's father signalling towards the door, where a man and a teenage girl were standing, looking around uncertainly. Alex always made sure to welcome any newcomers herself and she took the steps between the seats at a run.

'Hello. My name's Alex Jackson.' She paused to get her breath back and the girl's face broke into a grin.

'Hi. I'm Carys.'

Alex had hoped that Carys would come today, and she'd said that her father would be bringing her. She wondered whether Carys had told him that they'd already spoken.

The man held out his hand. 'I'm Ben Wheeler. I hear my daughter's been phoning you.'

'Dad...' Carys started to protest and Alex smiled at the man. Traces of grey in his hair, and lines around his eyes. His smile seemed weary, as if it was something he had to remember to do.

'We're always glad to hear from young people who might be interested in joining us.' She decided to tread lightly at first.

'Well, I don't know whether she's ready. She's having problems with the fit of her prosthesis...'

'Dad!' Carys frowned, obviously feeling that her father was intent on undermining her.

'That's not unusual. It sometimes takes a while to get things right. We can give some help and advice on that, and in the meantime perhaps I can introduce Carys to some of our members.'

'Right. Yes, that's…' Ben rubbed his hand across his head in a gesture of helplessness. 'Will you be all right on the steps, Carys?'

'I'm a physiotherapist; I'll make sure she doesn't fall.' Alex put on her most persuasive smile. 'Why don't you sit and watch—we'll be having more races soon.'

She gestured towards a seat, which just happened to be in front of Hayley's parents, and Ben nodded and sat down. As she turned, she saw Hayley's father leaning forward to introduce himself.

Carys was looking uncertainly at the steps running down in front of her. 'Shall we go round the other way? It's a bit further to walk, but there are no steps.'

'No. I think I can manage them.'

'Good girl. We'll do it together. Left leg first.' Alex tucked Carys's hand around her arm, ready to support her if she started to wobble, and Carys carefully lowered her prosthetic limb down the first step.

'I thought you were going to talk to him…' They'd got almost to the bottom of the steps, taking it slowly, one at a time, before Carys muttered the words at her.

Alex glanced over her shoulder. Ben had already swapped seats to sit with Hayley's parents, and a couple of the other parents had wandered over to introduce themselves. 'It's like we said on the phone, Carys…'

'Hi… You're Carys?' Leo was suddenly beside her, brimming with restless energy. Carys stared at him, momentarily forgetting all about the three more steps she had in front of her.

Alex waved Leo out of the way and he backed down the steps, giving Carys room to laboriously finish her descent. As soon as she was at the bottom, Carys turned to Leo, obviously deciding that she had a better chance of convincing him than she did Alex.

'I came for my dad. He's up there, talking to those people. Will *you* go and tell him?'

Leo was momentarily at a loss, glancing at Alex, who shook her head. 'I think it might be better to just allow him to talk to the people he's with for the time being.'

'But he'll listen to you—you're a doctor.' Carys was already treating him like a friend, venting her frustration at him. Alex supposed that a lot of people felt they knew Leo after listening to his voice on the radio, and that it must be something of a mixed blessing.

'What about showing him something? Show him that you can come here and make a few friends.' Leo was capitalising shamelessly on the artificial intimacy, moulding it into a real one.

Carys looked at Alex, clearly wanting her confirmation. This wasn't the time to indulge in hand-to-hand combat with Leo. Carys had told her that whatever her father said, her mother promptly took the opposite stance, and she must be pretty used to playing one off against the other. That was one of the problems she was facing.

'He's right.'

Leo shot her a surprised look and then warmed to his theme. 'Your dad's up there, talking to the other parents. They know exactly how he feels, and I think we ought to give him a chance to hear what they've got to say.'

'Yes.' Alex nodded her agreement, ignoring the amusement in Leo's eyes.

'Okay.' Carys shrugged. 'I suppose we could give it a go…'

'Yeah. Nice one.' Leo walked her slowly over to Hayley and Alice, making the introductions, and Alice shifted over one seat so that Carys could sit down in between them. Alex watched while the girls started to chat to each other.

She'd get Rhona to keep an eye on Carys while she got ready for the next race.

Which reminded her... 'If you're going to take part in the adults' race, then you'd better go and get changed, Leo.'

'Yeah. Sure thing.' His smile took on a teasingly confrontational edge. 'Get ready to be looking at my back all the way round.'

'In your dreams.'

He feigned a look of surprise. 'What happened to "Yes"? I was thinking for a moment there that you'd finally got around to realising that everything I say is right.'

'That was in your dreams too. Go and get changed. And prepare to be watching *my* back...' Alex turned, leaving him standing alone, and made her way to the women's changing rooms.

The thought of being able to watch Alex's back all the way round the arena, with no one to accuse him of staring at her, was tempting. Almost tempting enough to make him throw away any thoughts of making a race out of it and slot himself in nicely behind her. But then Alex seemed to see right through him, and she'd probably guess. And if she thought for one moment that he was letting her win, she'd be furious.

He consoled himself with watching her walk away now. Leo knew that each step using a prosthetic leg took more energy than one with your own two legs. Just a little, but over the course of a day it all added up. The controlled, graceful sway of her body showed both the kids and their parents how much they could achieve, what they were working so hard towards.

Everything she did was a delicious reminder of their kiss. That tangled web of so many delights, which even the sharp tang of guilt couldn't drive from his mind.

It was his own fault. If he hadn't surrendered to the

moment, he wouldn't be plagued by it now. Nor would he have to keep telling himself that it mustn't happen again.

'Leo, Evangeline asked me to come and find you.' He turned and saw Evie's minder standing next to him.

'Yeah? Anything the matter?'

'Arielle's not well.'

'One of her headaches?' Evie had told him that, since the meningitis, Arielle had suffered from debilitating headaches and dizzy spells, which seemed to come on with no warning.

'Yep. She's in the first aid room.'

'Right. Where's that?'

Arielle was lying on the bed in the first aid room, her eyes closed, Evie at her side. When Leo opened the door, she ushered him backwards into the corridor, closing the door quietly behind them.

'How is she?'

'Done for this afternoon. She needs to go back to the hotel and sleep this off. Will you have a look at her though, Leo? We've got the name of a doctor here but I've never met him, and I trust you…'

'Would you like me to come back to the hotel with you?' The words fell heavy from his lips. This afternoon had been special in so many ways, and it felt suddenly as if he was ripping himself away.

'Oh, Leo, would you? I'm not sure whether the flight over here might have affected her…'

'Of course. I've finished everything I need to do here.' The lie sounded convincing enough to his ears, and Evie accepted it immediately. He'd been spending too much time with Alex lately. She was the only one who would have questioned him on it.

'I feel so bad about leaving now. So does Arielle—those kids have so much heart.'

'Why don't you stay? I'll take care of Arielle and stay

with her until you get back.' It was the obvious solution. Leo's place was with anyone who needed him, not with Alex, however loath he was to admit that.

'Would you mind? Arielle asked me to stay, but I can't have you going with her while I'm here...'

Leo laid his hand on her arm. 'It's not a problem. These kids deserve all the support we can give them. Does Arielle have a copy of her medical records with her?'

'Yes, it's on the dresser in her room. Along with her medication.'

'I'll find them.'

Evie took the microphone from his hand and wound her arms around his shoulders, kissing him on the cheek. Leo hugged her. She was acknowledged as one of the most beautiful women in the world and no man in his right mind could fail to notice that. Only all he could think about was that she wasn't Alex.

'Do me a favour, would you, Evie?'

'Of course.'

'The little guy, Sam. Red hair and freckles—he's been following you around all afternoon.'

'He's such a cute kid. What about him?'

'Alex told me he loves being in the races, even if he always comes last. Make sure he gets a cheer when he runs, eh?' Leo knew he'd get one anyway but he'd so wanted to be there, cheering for Sam himself.

'Of course I will. You're not the only one who can work a crowd, you know.'

'I know. Now, get out of my way, will you. I've got a patient to see.'

Alex was eating a sandwich at her desk, in lieu of Sunday lunch, when her phone rang. That was Leo all over. She'd waited up last night, hoping he would call after leaving so abruptly, and he hadn't, and now that she'd managed not to think about him for five consecutive minutes he'd called.

'Hi. Where are you?'

'At my office.'

'Had lunch yet?'

'Yes, I've just eaten. How's Arielle?'

'Much better. Some people do suffer from headaches after they've had meningitis. It's a concern, of course, and Arielle naturally gets worried by it, but it's unusual for meningitis to recur. I called in this morning and she was fine.'

'That's good. I was wondering… I'd like to send her something, just to say thank you for coming and that I'm glad she's feeling better. I did think of flowers, but I guess she and Evie probably have whole roomfuls already…' Perhaps Leo could suggest something. Alex hoped he could because she had absolutely no idea what would be appropriate.

He chuckled. 'Yeah, it's a bit like Kew Gardens in there. I don't know how Evie stands it; I was sneezing all evening.' He paused for a moment to think. 'Do you have any photos from yesterday? I saw Rhona brandishing a camera.'

'We should have. Hold on, I'll look and see whether she's uploaded them onto the server yet.' Alex opened the images folder and saw a new folder with yesterday's date on it. 'Yes, they're there.'

'Why don't you pick out some nice ones and send them with a personal note? That's something I'm sure they'd both really appreciate.'

'It's not very much…'

'It'll be perfect.' Leo's tone suggested that the matter was dealt with and that he was already moving on. 'You'll be there for a while?'

'I think I'll pop out now and get a card to send with the photos. And I'll need a thumb drive too. I'll be back in half an hour.'

'In that case, I'll see you then.'

That question also appeared to be dealt with in Leo's

mind because he didn't wait for an answer before hanging up. Alex stared at her phone.

'Yes, half an hour's convenient for me, Leo.' She dropped the phone back onto her desk. It really didn't matter if it wasn't, because it appeared that Leo would be coming anyway.

The card for Arielle sat in front of her on the desk and Alex was holding her pen, ready to write something as soon as inspiration struck her, when a quiet knock sounded at the door and it swung open.

She was getting used to the fact that all doors were open to Leo, and didn't bother to ask how he'd got into the building without pressing the night bell. Probably a couple of the people downstairs, who were busy preparing for a case in court tomorrow.

And who wouldn't let Leo in anywhere? He always looked as if he belonged, wherever he went. He'd made some concession to this being a Sunday, dark jeans and a charcoal sweater, his blond hair slightly more rumpled than usual. Of course, it was all artifice. Leo was never really off-duty; it just suited him to look as if he was from time to time.

'I thought you might need something to keep you going. Ready for a Tellurian cocktail?'

So he remembered. She couldn't attach too much importance to that, because she'd then have to attach an equal importance to the fact that she remembered too. And that particular episode of their lives was over now. They'd kissed it goodbye.

'I'm not sure I'll be ready for another one of those for at least another ten years.' It was tempting, though. Leo was tempting.

'They've improved a great deal.' He sauntered over to her desk, revealing what he'd been holding behind his back.

Two crystal glasses that shone in the feeble afternoon light and a cocktail shaker.

'I seem to remember that pouring them down the sink was about the only thing that anyone could have done to redeem them.'

'Harsh, Alex.' He laughed. 'Don't you think that anything can be redeemed with a little work?'

Maybe. But Leo was working on all the wrong things.

'I'm not sure blue's my colour...'

'Blue is everyone's colour. Particularly yours...'

He opened the cocktail shaker and poured a measure into each glass. Maybe it was her imagination but the blue liquid was slightly less vivid than the original Tellurian cocktails. It actually looked quite intriguing.

Leo put a glass into her hand and sat down in the chair next to her desk. 'We should make a toast. To all we can achieve.' He tipped his glass towards hers.

'Yes. All we can achieve.' It sounded like a good toast. Alex took an exploratory sip from her glass.

'Oh! That's quite nice.' She took another sip. 'Actually, it's very nice.' Not too much sweetness, but just enough to temper the bite.

He smiled. 'Want to take a guess?'

'Hmm. Blue curaçao, obviously.' She took another sip. 'I'm not sure what else, though...' If there was another spirit, it had to be colourless. 'You haven't laced this with vodka, have you?'

He arched one eyebrow. 'No. I'm going for taste, not trying to get you drunk.'

'That's good to hear.' Alex took another sip, just to show him that she could handle it. 'So what *are* you here for, Leo?'

'Would you believe Sunday afternoon cocktails?'

'No. You said it yourself, Leo. There's no such thing as just drinks. What are you here for?'

'To apologise for rushing off like that yesterday.'

'You don't have to apologise. I know you had to go. I'm just happy that Arielle's all right.'

'Yeah. I guess it was my loss. There's something else.' He reached into his back pocket and brought out a folded envelope. 'I was talking to Alice yesterday.'

'Yes?'

'She says that running blades aren't automatically supplied on the NHS, and that her family can't afford to pay for one. You've been helping her to put applications in for funding, but she's not been successful yet so she's got herself a job.'

Alex quirked her mouth downwards. 'Yes, that's right. She stacks shelves in the supermarket a couple of evenings a week but that's not going to cover it. I'm going to have to think of something…'

Leo leaned forward, handing her the envelope. Alex opened it and drew out a folded sheet of notepaper. When she opened it a cheque fell out.

She read the letter carefully. Leo's donation to the charity was to be anonymous, and it was to be used to buy Alice's running blade. Alex caught her breath, blinking back the tears.

'Is that enough?'

'It's more than enough. This would pay for her blade and the upkeep for a couple of years.' It was what Alex had been praying for. Her fingers shook as she put the cheque down on the desk.

'This is…' She thought carefully about what she wanted to say. 'This is a wonderful act of generosity, Leo. Thank you.'

'It's my pleasure.'

'And you've tied my hands. I have to accept it.'

A flicker of doubt showed in his face. 'I sense a *but* coming.'

Alex took a deep breath. She owed it to Alice to accept

the cheque, but she owed something to Leo too. 'But I want you to think about why you're doing this, Leo.'

'Why would I have to do that? You said yesterday that Alice has a lot of potential, and she's never going to be able to fulfil that without help.' His lip curled in disbelief. 'What more do you want?'

'We have a lot of people who support us, and we ask a lot of them. I have a duty of care to them as well as our clients.'

'You think I can't afford this?'

'I know you can from a financial point of view. My worry is that…that it's not going to buy you…' The word stuck in her throat.

'Buy me what?'

'Forgiveness.'

The shock in his eyes was palpable. For a moment Alex thought he was going to snatch the cheque up from her desk and walk out. What had she done?

Then he leaned back in his seat, rubbing his face with his hands. 'Why do you have to make everything so damn difficult, Alex?'

'Because…' Because she cared about Leo. If this money was all it took to allow him to forgive himself, it would be a bargain. But it wasn't, and he'd just keep on giving until he was too worn out to give any more.

'Because if I don't say this I'd be letting Alice down. And myself.' Alex reached forward and took his hand. Felt his fingers curl around hers in a delicious artifice of an embrace.

'Say it then.' His gaze was dark, suddenly. Entirely hers.

'I want you to know that this gift is not because you have some kind of debt to pay; it's because you're a good man and you have a good heart.'

'You don't understand, Alex.' Something about the way he said it told her that he might just be coaxed into explaining.

'Then tell me.'

He leaned forward, raising her hand to his lips in the parody of a kiss. For a moment Alex thought this was his way of letting her go, but he kept hold of her, clasping her fingers tightly between both his hands now.

'This is between you and me. No one else must know.'

'Yes. I understand.' What could be this bad? Alex swallowed hard, trying to prepare herself.

'My parents think that Joel overdosed by mistake. It's a possibility that gives them some comfort and I can't take that away from them. But it was no mistake. He called me.'

'But…you didn't speak to him, right? You don't know what he was going to say.'

Leo shook his head wearily. 'He called me five times, Alex, and I missed all of those calls. If that isn't a cry for help I don't know what is.'

She stared at him, numb with shock. Alex couldn't imagine how that must feel. How he must constantly be going back to that, wondering whether he could have saved his own twin brother's life.

'It was the last weekend before I went home for Christmas, and my girlfriend wanted to go away somewhere. I switched off my phone, and left my brother alone on the one night he really needed me.'

'But… Leo, people miss calls all the time…'

'I know. And usually it doesn't matter all that much but…' He shrugged. 'All I want is to give Alice the opportunity to run. I'm not looking to buy forgiveness because there isn't any.'

There was nothing she could say. It was too cruel, too heartbreaking and there were no answers to it. Alice came to her rescue.

'What Alice said…'

'I know. I heard her. If you just try hard enough you can do anything. It's a great thought and, coming from a kid like her who's had so much to contend with already, it's inspirational. But she doesn't know everything, Alex. You and I know that there are some things you can't do, and we just have to learn to live with that.'

'Won't you think about it?'

He shook his head, letting go of her hand. 'No, I'm not going to think about it. Because I can't change anything and if I thought about it too much I'd just be a mess. And there are things I have to do.'

She was losing him. He poured the rest of the contents of the cocktail shaker into her glass and drained his. Then he got to his feet.

'You're going?'

'Like I said. Things to do. Paperwork.'

'Can't you do it another time? We could go for something to eat, or catch a movie...'

He smiled. That relentless, charming smile which hid so much. 'Can I take a rain check? I really do have to work.'

He'd obviously forgotten that he'd asked her out to lunch first. Perhaps it was something that had suddenly come up, but Alex doubted it. Leo was drawing back, resorting to the tried and tested formula of not having time to think about anything.

'Yes, okay. Rain check.' She wondered what freak of nature was going to have to occur before the weather changed enough to induce Leo to change his mind.

'Fantastic. See you tomorrow...' He threw the words over his shoulder and walked out of the door.

CHAPTER TEN

IT WAS AS if nothing had happened between them. Leo was smiling and relaxed when he arrived at the radio station, taking the receipt for the cheque that she handed him with a nod but without saying anything.

If shaking him hard would have worked then Alex was quite prepared to do it. But it wouldn't. Leo's urbane charm wasn't a reflection that everything was right in his world. It was a fallback position, and he hung onto it just as grimly as anyone else might hold onto anger.

Their hour on-air together flew. Leo was the ultimate back seat driver, supportive when he needed to be and letting her talk when she was on a roll and knew what she wanted to say. His gaze connected with hers as they said their goodbyes for tonight and went off-air and they both heaved a sigh, flopping back into their seats in unison.

'Fabulous!' Justin burst into the studio. 'Great hour, both of you.'

Leo gestured towards Alex, chuckling. 'Nothing to do with me. That was the Alex Jackson Medical Hour you just heard.'

'You handled the sex beautifully…' Justin was in full flow, and Leo raised his eyebrows.

'Actually, we were talking about body awareness issues. You must have been listening to something else, Justin.'

'Sex, body awareness… It's all the same thing…' Justin stopped short as Leo shot him a frown. 'Okay, well, perhaps it isn't. Great body awareness, then. And it was a fantastic hour, just *like* sex on the airwaves.'

Alex had felt that too. A meeting of minds instead of bodies, but nonetheless a lot like sex. But Leo, gentleman to the last, wasn't having it.

'Do me a favour and save the sex on the airwaves for the Jazz Hour, will you? Have you got the call-backs?'

Justin produced an envelope from the file he was carrying. 'Here you go. Rather a lot of them, I'm afraid…'

'That's good. We want a lot.' Alex spoke up and Leo chuckled.

'Want to go halves?' Leo opened the envelope, drawing out a dozen sheets of paper, stapled together.

'Yes, thanks. I don't think I can get through all of those tomorrow.'

He nodded, counting the sheets out and dividing them, pulling the back half from the staple and putting them into the envelope.

'How's the piece going for the Community Affairs programme?' Leo asked Justin.

'Very good. We've put together what you did, along with a few bits from the second half of the afternoon. It'll be a fifteen minute slot.'

'That's great. Thanks.'

Leo waited for Justin to leave, and Alex saw him switch the voice link to the control room off. 'Despite all appearances, Justin's one of the best radio producers around. I'm lucky to be working with him.'

'But you don't tell him that. Just to keep him on his toes.'

'I told him. We were both a bit drunk at the time, and he told me I was radio gold and I told him he was the kind of producer that could turn a sow's ear into a silk purse. We don't mention it, of course.'

'Of course not. That would be kiss and tell.'

Leo chuckled. 'I wasn't drunk enough to kiss him. We're a good team though, and he knows it.'

'He keeps you focused and you keep him honest?' Alex wondered whether Leo would admit to being the heart behind the show.

'There you go again. Making out I'm better than I really am.' He got to his feet. That way of his, of closing a conversation before it got too uncomfortably close to reality.

Leo walked over to the door and waited and, when she didn't follow him, he raised his eyebrows. 'What?'

'Nothing.' She smiled back at him innocently, her heart pounding. This time, Leo wasn't going to walk away, not before she'd done what she'd decided to do. And then maybe *she'd* be the one to walk away.

He heaved a sigh and threw himself back into his seat. 'All right. I'll wait.'

Alex rummaged in her bag, and pulled out the thumb drive. Leaning over, she put it into his hand. 'The photos…'

'For our website?'

'No, I gave a set to Justin, before you arrived. These are for you.' She rose, planting her hands on the arms of his chair. He looked up at her steadily, obviously waiting for her to make the next move.

'I thought the show was great tonight. Thank you.' She met his gaze, staring him straight in the eye as she said it. Then she leaned in. 'So was the sex. Really enjoyed it.'

'Does that mean you're coming back for coffee?'

Alex straightened. 'Thanks, but no. I've got to go, and I asked your production assistant to make sure my car was waiting as soon as the programme ended.' She turned, grabbed her coat and bag and walked away from him.

It was snowing again, the light flakes taking on the shape of the wind, outside his window. Leo had taken a shower and was sprawled on his bed, his laptop in front of him, looking at the photographs.

He could almost taste the day again. Hear the cheers as Hayley passed the finishing line. See Alex running up to Alice and hugging her, ready for them both to smile into the camera. And there were snapshots of what had happened after he'd left. Little Sam, lagging behind the rest, the winners of his race turning to egg him on towards the finishing line. Evie, picking the little guy up, his arms held aloft, in front of a crowd that had risen to its feet and were applauding him.

He rolled over onto his back, staring at the ceiling. Alex had given him these photographs because she knew they'd touch his heart and in the stubborn belief that there was something of value there.

But their kiss had told him all he needed to know. It would be so easy, so sweet, to lose himself in her arms. But then the guilt would kick in and tear it all apart.

He'd work it out. Somehow strike a balance, learn to love her as a friend, and that would be enough. He'd start tomorrow, because tonight he wanted to look at the photographs, one more time.

'Hey. What are you doing on Saturday?' As usual, Leo launched straight into what he was intending to say without bothering with any preliminaries.

'Nothing very much. I was going to drive down to my parents' and stay the night, ready for the climbing wall on Sunday.' Almost twenty-four hours without having heard from Leo forced Alex to ask, 'You are coming on Sunday, aren't you?'

'Wouldn't miss it.' He neglected the obvious, not mentioning that he could be called away at any time. 'I've got a couple of tickets for a media do on Saturday evening; the radio station's got a table. Will you come?'

'I'm… What sort of do?' Alex thought furiously for some kind of excuse. It sounded much more like the kind of function that Leo would go to, and Alex suspected that she'd be like a fish out of water.

'It's a dinner dance. A lot of the right people are going, and it'll be good to get your name out there.'

'Out where…?'

Leo chuckled. 'Figure of speech. You get to meet people; they get to meet you. It's a great opportunity.'

It was a great opportunity to make a complete and utter fool of herself. 'I don't know, Leo. I'd have to drive all the way down to Sussex afterwards.'

'Not necessarily. It's being held in South London, and I can come and pick you up and take you there. Then afterwards we'll go to my place, down in Surrey, and grab a few hours' sleep. We can get up early on Sunday and drive down to Sussex then.'

That would work… Alex shook her head. She couldn't believe that she was even thinking about it.

'It'll be fun. Chance to dress up a bit…'

That was exactly what was bothering her. 'Well, to be honest, I'm not sure I have anything suitable to wear. This do is black tie, is it?'

'Yeah. Well, if that's all that's bothering you, then that's perfect. We can go shopping…'

Oh, no. She could see it now, having to try about a million different dresses on while Leo waited outside the changing room. He'd probably talk her into something that she normally wouldn't wear and then offer to pay for it, so she couldn't change her mind later.

'No, on second thoughts I can probably find something lurking at the back of my wardrobe.'

'Great. Last year it was quite formal—most of the women wore long dresses. You can't go wrong with black…'

'I'll bear it in mind. And... Well, thanks for the invitation. And I guess I'll see you on Saturday.' That was another five days, and Alex could say the words with only a minor murmur of panic.

'Something lurking in the back of your wardrobe?' Rhona looked up from her desk as Alex put her phone down. 'Going somewhere nice?'

'Leo's asked me to a dinner dance on Saturday. He says it would be good to meet some people.'

Rhona nodded. 'He's right.'

'Yes, I know he is. What am I going to wear, though?' Rhona had been through the contents of Alex's wardrobe often enough. Some summer dresses, a few smart separates and a suit; the rest was all casual wear. None of that was going to do.

'Looks as if you'll be hitting the shops. Or Mum can run something up for you, if you like.' Rhona's mother had been a seamstress and still made most of her own and her daughter's clothes. Rhona would bring a bolt of fabric into the office, and a couple of days later would appear in something that was entirely unique and usually stupendous.

'Thanks. I don't want to put her to any trouble.'

'You know it's no trouble. Why don't you go and have a look around at what's in the shops now, and if there's something you like that's fine. If not, you've got some clue about what you *would* like.'

What Alex really would like was to look effortlessly glamorous, the way Evie did. Have Leo gasp and compliment her dress. 'I think I'll settle for just not looking out of place.'

'Whatever. Just go. Once you've got a few ideas you'll feel better.'

Alex didn't feel any better. She'd been into three or four of the big stores in Oxford Street and picked up a whole string of black dresses, putting most of them back down again. The ones she'd tried on all had something wrong with them—too fussy, too revealing. And black just didn't seem to suit her.

She flopped down on one of the comfortable sofas next to the entrance of the changing room. This was all a disaster. She was going to be scouring the shops for the next three days, then she'd panic and get just anything. Then feel even worse because Leo would undoubtedly look immaculate and good enough to eat.

Alex looked at her watch. An hour before closing time. She could either look at everything again, to make sure there was nothing she'd missed, or give up and go to the in-store café. Maybe if she came back tomorrow evening, after work…

Then she saw it. Alex got up wearily, walking over to the mannequin and looking at the price ticket. That wasn't too much. If it fitted…

She caught up the dress and walked to the changing room. It wasn't going to fit. The neck wouldn't look right. There was going to be something the matter with it, the way that there was something the matter with all the others.

But it *did* fit. It was simple, plain and, when Alex left her cubicle to try walking up and down a little, the skirts were wide enough and didn't cling around her legs. She stopped in front of a long mirror by the entrance to the changing room and one of the sales assistants looked up from the desk.

'That looks nice…'

'I'm…not sure.' Alex stared at herself in the mirror.

'No, it's lovely.' A woman on her way into the changing room stopped, laying an armful of clothes on the counter. 'It really suits you. Understated but it looks classy.'

Classy was just what she wanted. Alex nodded her thanks and went back to the cubicle, pulling out her phone.

'Rhona… I need your help…'

* * *

Leo couldn't deny that he was looking forward to Saturday evening. By the time he'd showered and dressed, he could almost taste his excitement. He took one look in the mirror and gave himself a nod of approval. He'd do. Neat and unremarkable, his attire designed to allow the woman on his arm all the attention.

Not that Alex needed him for that; she dazzled all by herself. She looked great in anything because it was her smile that everyone noticed. Alex was one of those women who outshone anything that she could possibly be wearing.

He picked up the keys for his SUV, parked next to his saloon car in the garage downstairs. The past few days had been wet, drizzle alternating with snow, and the track which led to his house in Surrey was likely to be muddy. Patting his pockets, checking that he had everything, he let himself out of the flat and called the lift.

He found Alex's name on the console by the main entrance to her block of flats and pressed her buzzer. It was oddly gratifying that she answered almost immediately, buzzing him inside. He walked up the stairs and found her door. He'd been fantasising about what she might wear all the way here, and had decided that Alex would go for the understated. Black probably, figure-hugging without being showily tight, and classy. Definitely classy.

She opened the front door wide and he felt his mouth suddenly too dry to utter the compliment that he'd had waiting. His feet were rooted to the spot and only his eyes seemed to have any power of movement.

'You look…' Completely and utterly dumbfounding.

She flushed pink, a trace of awkwardness on her face. 'Too much…?'

Far too much. How on earth did she think that he was going to wrench his gaze away from her and talk coherently to anyone else tonight?

'You look stupendous.' He took one step towards her, almost afraid to go any nearer.

She was a deeper pink now, but the uncertainty had given way to a smile. 'You like it?'

Like it? Was she entirely mad? Her dress was jewel-green, simply cut, with sheer fabric at the neckline and covering her arms. Shimmering, iridescent sequins spilled from the right side of the neckline, spreading out across her shoulder and down her sleeve, with another trail meandering down across her breast and disappearing in the soft folds of her skirts. Her hair was swept up, and he could see silver pins anchoring the soft curls. Not quite Tara's silver dagger pins, but reminiscent of them. She stepped back from the doorway and as she moved the sequins glimmered blue and green and the silver tracery on the cuff bracelets she wore sparkled.

Many women had dressed up for him before, but no one had ever done anything like this. This was a shared secret, a nod to their past, which only he got. Everyone else would simply think she was the most beautiful woman in the room.

'It's stunning.' *She* was stunning. Leo stepped into the hallway, leaning towards her. 'If you tell me you have an immobility gun strapped to your leg, I think I'm going to faint.'

She laughed. 'No, it would spoil the line of the skirt. I am armed, though.'

'And ready to go?' He'd been wondering whether he'd get to see her flat, but now Leo didn't care. All he wanted to look at was her.

'Yes.' She picked up her coat, along with a small silver clutch bag, and indicated a large zipped bag. As he bent to pick it up, Leo caught a subtle breath of her scent.

He held out his arm and she took it. 'Armed how?'

'That would be telling...' Her eyes flashed with mischievous humour, and another layer added itself to the fantasy. 'The first strategy is always surprise.'

Leo wondered whether he should have thought to bring a weapon as well. Every guy in the room was going to be fighting for her attention tonight. But he had the advantage. He'd bet everything he had that Alex was the kind of woman who always went home with the guy she came with.

CHAPTER ELEVEN

HE LIKED THE DRESS. What had started out as a bit of fun had turned into uncertainty over whether the idea was really going to work. Rhona and her mum had egged her on, and the three of them had spent an evening laughing over the application of sequins to the dress that Alex had bought. Then the terror had set in. But when she'd seen approval in Leo's eyes she'd been able to breathe again.

It was an hour's drive to the hotel where the dinner dance was being held, and Leo seemed to know that she was still nervous. He always knew how to calm her though, and when she walked into the enormous banqueting hall, hanging on tightly to his arm, it seemed less daunting than she'd thought it would be.

He found their table and Alex was relieved to see Justin there, along with a few other faces she knew. Leo was on good form, quietly attentive but at the same time laughing and joking with everyone, and she began to enjoy herself.

A meal was served and then came the speeches, which were mercifully short. Then the diners began to meander away from their tables, circulating and greeting friends. Leo seemed to know almost everyone here and he was clearly on a mission, steering Alex from one group to another, introducing her and working her charity seamlessly into each conversation.

'What a nice man…' Alex had spoken for a while to a

white-haired man who had asked a number of perceptive questions about her work and listened carefully to her answers.

'He's on the board of one of the biggest publishing organisations in the country.' Leo leaned in towards her, whispering the name into her ear.

'Really?' Alex's hand flew to her mouth and she felt her ears begin to redden.

Leo grinned. 'Just as well I didn't tell you before. You would have clammed up, and smiled and nodded instead of being your usual interesting self.'

'Well…yes. I'll give you that. I *would* have clammed up.'

'And he didn't get where he is by standing grinning at people.'

Alex wrinkled her nose. 'Do you think I was too…?'

'You were perfect. Would you like to dance?'

Yes. She'd really like to dance with Leo. Have his arm around her waist, feel his body moving against hers. Maybe that was asking just a little bit too much of an already great evening, though.

'I'd like to find the ladies' room first…'

He gestured over his shoulder. 'That way.'

She moved through the press of people, finding herself in a large, comfortable lobby. Two women were already there, standing by the mirrors, gossiping. Alex paid no attention to them until she was about to leave, and walked over to the mirror to check her lipstick.

'I glimpsed Leo on the way in. Looking as mouth-watering as ever.' The woman in the blue dress was talking rather too loudly to ignore.

'Is he? I'll have to go and strike up a conversation!' the black dress replied.

'Fancy a threesome?' Blue dress laughed unattractively.

'I don't mind sharing, darling. Leo's never struck me as the type for that kind of thing, though.'

Alex pressed her lips together, staring at her reflection

in the mirror, willing it to be impassive. Going across to the women and reminding them that Leo was a person and not just a pretty face probably wouldn't be all that tactful. She was meant to be putting on her lipstick, not listening to their conversation.

'Did you hear his show on Monday? I was playing it in the car on the way down here. Marvellous chemistry. Apparently he's brought her along tonight.'

'Really?'

'Yes—' Blue dress broke off, but Alex could see her reflection in the mirror, mouthing to her companion. *She's only got one leg. Fancy bringing her to a dance.*

'Poor thing.' Black dress shuddered ostentatiously. 'Are you still thinking of making Leo an offer?'

'I tried. Not interested. I offered him twice whatever he's getting at the radio station and he turned me down flat. Said that he wanted to concentrate on serious medical issues, whatever that means, and that he was happy working with Justin. *Justin*, for goodness' sake…'

'Shame. With his ratings, he could do anything.'

'Yes, and, between you and me, I need something. We're already having to fight for our advertising revenue…'

Alex glared at the women's reflections but they didn't notice. It wasn't the first time she'd heard any of the barbs they'd thrown at her and it wouldn't be the last, but they still rankled. How dare these women call her a *poor thing*? How dare they think that having had part of her leg amputated was so shameful they couldn't even say it? And how dare they assume that she couldn't dance with Leo if she wanted to?

They weren't worth her time, or her anger. She repeated the words over in her head a couple of times, looking at herself in the mirror. Then she put her lipstick back into her bag and made for the door, even returning the smile that blue dress aimed in her direction as she walked past them.

She turned the corner which led to the door and heard

one of the women speak again. 'Don't you just *love* that dress? I wonder where she got it.'

'And did you see her shoes? So pretty.'

'I must get a pair like that. She looks so graceful, and I can hardly walk in these heels…they're killing me…'

Leo turned when she put her hand on his arm, smiling down at her. Alex reached out, running her fingers down the side of his lapel, not caring how unmistakably possessive the gesture was.

'Do you still want to dance?'

He grinned. 'I'd love to dance.'

He took her hand, leading her towards the dance floor. She felt suddenly both too warm and too cold, her fingers almost icy in his hand, her cheeks hot. Alex wondered how many other people here were looking at her, thinking exactly the same as the women in the ladies' room.

When he laid his hand on her back she smiled up at him, but her whole body felt stiff and tense. Leo took a couple of steps and she moved with him, like an automaton.

'What's the matter?' The tenderness in his gaze seemed to bore into her.

'Nothing.'

'Really?' He was guiding her over to the very edge of the dance floor. He was going to stop and go and sit down. And then everyone would be looking at her, thinking she couldn't dance.

'No, Leo. I want to stay here…' She heard the pleading tone in her voice.

'Okay. But what's up?'

'I… It's nothing. People just say things without thinking.' Leo wouldn't understand this. He was a doctor and he took it so much for granted that she was more than her disability that he probably didn't even imagine that people could be that cruel.

'Okay, so it's nothing. Care to share it, all the same? In the interests of research.'

'Research?'

'Yeah. Crass things that people say. I'm always interested in that kind of thing.'

She couldn't help smiling up at him. 'You won't like it...'

'Well, clearly you don't either, so we can not like it together. Call it a bonding exercise.' His hand had been resting lightly on her back but suddenly he drew her in, trapping her against him. His other hand curled around hers.

'It was just two women, talking in the ladies' room. They started off by saying they wouldn't mind a threesome with you.'

She felt his chest heave against hers as he choked suddenly. 'Tell me you managed to knock that idea on the head. Please.'

'I couldn't. They weren't actually talking to me. I overheard.'

'Okay, I get it. You're staring in the mirror, fiddling with your hair, and they're off in a corner somewhere gossiping.' His lips twitched into a smile. 'Nice bit of undercover work there, Lieutenant. Did you get them with the hairpins?'

'No. They're actually not very sharp.' Leo had this knack of making her feel better. Or maybe it was the way he was holding her. Almost an embrace, moving slowly along with the music.

'So they've escaped for the time being. Never mind; we'll get them later. Continue with the surveillance report, please, Lieutenant.'

Alex couldn't help laughing. 'They'd heard the programme. They called me a *poor thing* and wanted to know why you'd brought me along tonight, when I obviously couldn't dance with you.'

Anger flashed in his eyes, and she felt his body stiffen

against hers. Then he puffed out a breath. 'And you didn't kick them?'

'I felt like it. But one of them said she'd made you an offer, for twice what you were earning now...'

Understanding dawned in his eyes. 'I know who you mean. Trust me, Alex, Clara Goodwin is seriously bad news. Three-quarters of the industry wouldn't even give her the time of day, let alone work for her. Anyway, it makes no difference, even if she'd made me the best offer in the world, you still should have kicked her.'

'It might have been a bit unfair. A prosthetic leg can give you a bit of a wallop, you know.'

'All the same. I'm disappointed in you.' He leaned in, his lips touching her ear. 'You are the most gorgeous woman in this room. You're intelligent and kind, and you dance beautifully. And even if you didn't, I'd still be proud that you agreed to come here with me tonight.'

Alex felt herself relax against him. 'That's nice of you.'

'I'm never nice, you know that.' He increased the rhythm of the dance a little, and Alex felt herself follow. 'What *is* nice is that you've finally loosened up. Any chance of letting me lead now?'

'I didn't realise I wasn't...' He raised his eyebrows, and Alex grinned back at him. 'Okay, maybe you're right. Take the helm, Captain.'

'My pleasure. Hang on, we have incoming on the starboard bow.'

His sudden turn almost lifted her off her feet, making her skirts float out behind her. It was like letting go without there being any danger of stumbling, because Leo was there.

They danced in silence for a while, their bodies moving together, staring into each other's eyes. Leo was good at this. He made it feel like sex should be, and very seldom was. A pure indulgence. Lost in his arms and yet there, right with him. Letting him lead and yet feeling him react to each movement of hers.

'So...' He pursed his lips thoughtfully, mischief flashing in his eyes. 'Am I correct in thinking that you're using me?'

'Absolutely. I'm showing the whole room that I can dance all night if I want to.'

'Good. Go for it.'

'But of course you're using me too.' He raised his eyebrows and she grinned at him. 'Those two women are out there somewhere, looking for a threesome...'

'Don't! You're going to have to stay right where you are until I manage to *un*-think that. And I warn you, it might take a while.'

'Good. Go for it.' She could do this all night. And then sleep for a while and do it all over again. But, since that wasn't going to happen, she'd make the best of it while she could.

Leo had tried to hide his anger, but he couldn't. How *dared* Clara Goodwin make Alex feel that she was anything less than perfect? Raising his hand to any woman was out of the question, but he might be persuaded to hold her still while Alex punched her.

And what made him angriest of all was that it wasn't the first time, and it was unlikely to be the last. Maybe it had been a good thing that he was unable to hide how he felt about that. She was so protective of the kids in her charge, so positive and encouraging on the radio, that it was sometimes easy to forget that she had feelings too, and that the careless cruelty of others still hurt her.

There was a measure of safety here, on the dance floor. Alex was nestled against him and the world seemed right. As if nothing could touch them for a while.

Not long enough, though. After two dances he found that a number of the people he'd introduced her to earlier wanted to continue their conversations with Alex on the dance floor, and he gave her up. This was what she was here for, to make new contacts.

Finally he got her back. 'Do you want to sit for a while?' He wondered if she would admit it to him if she did, but she did so without hesitation.

'Yes, I wouldn't mind. Shall we give this one a miss?'

'Good idea. There's always the next one.'

But there wasn't a next one. As they walked together over to the drinks buffet, he saw a commotion at the corner of the room. A couple of people looked around, and then someone pointed straight at him. A man dressed in the dark red jacket which was the livery of the hotel started to push his way towards him.

'Dr Leo Cross?'

'Yes?'

'There's been an incident in the kitchen, sir. We need a doctor. It's an emergency.'

'All right. I'll come now.' Leo shot an apologetic look at Alex and she nodded, disappointment showing on her face. He followed the man through the crush of people, cursing whatever twist of fate had called him away from her a second time. Last Saturday had been unfortunate. This Saturday was beginning to look as if some malevolent force of nature had it in for him.

It couldn't be helped. This was what he'd signed up for when he became a doctor. Alex would understand. She had to.

The man led him from the banqueting hall and along a service corridor. 'What's happened?'

'One of the cooks, sir. He's cut his finger off. I've got someone calling an ambulance, but we can't stop the bleeding.'

'You have a medical kit?'

'Yes, there's one in the kitchen. Gets used quite a bit so we keep it well stocked.'

'And you have Health and Safety procedures for dealing with blood spillage?' It sounded as if there was going to be a fair bit of blood, and there was no way of knowing whether there was a risk of infection.

'Yes, they're in place. I'll get everyone out of there and cleaned up.'

'Good.'

They rounded a corner and then hurried through a door, which led to a large kitchen. Even though it was late, there were still half a dozen people here who were currently all gathered around a man who was sitting on the floor in the corner. A trail of blood led from one of the nearby work benches, and was beginning to pool around his legs.

'Everyone move back, please.' Leo took off his jacket, rolling up his sleeves and grabbing a pair of gloves from the large medical box which stood open on the counter. The group around the man scattered, everyone craning to see what was happening.

The man was doubled over, cradling his injured hand and moaning loudly. Leo knew that he must be in a great deal of pain, but there was nothing he could do about that. He carried a medical bag in his car, but that didn't include the drugs he needed now.

'Alan…' The man's name was sewn onto his tunic, above the breast pocket. 'Alan, I'm a doctor. Let me see your hand.'

Leo reached for Alan's arm but he batted him away, rocking back and forth, blood leaking from the towel that was wound around his hand.

'Alan… Look at me.' Leo put his hand on the side of Alan's face, tipping it towards his. 'I'm a doctor. I know it hurts, but you need to show me your hand.'

This time, Alan didn't resist when he reached for his arm. Gingerly, Leo unwound the towel and saw that the first phalanx of his index finger had been completely severed, leaving only a half-inch stump. Blood pulsed from the wound, dripping onto the floor.

'Alan, I need you to hold your arm up.' Leo elevated the man's hand and Alan swore at him, moaning with pain. Finding the position of the main veins in his wrist, Leo pressed hard, and the flow of blood began to slow.

'Can someone get me…?' He looked up and saw six pairs of eyes staring blankly at him. He needed someone to help him and it didn't look as if any of this lot were going to volunteer. Then he saw a flash of green by the door and a seventh pair of eyes, honey-brown. Alex was hurrying towards him.

CHAPTER TWELVE

'I NEED SOME water and plenty of gauze. Put a pair of gloves on first. And be careful—there's blood on the floor; don't slip on it.'

Leo bit his tongue. Alex worked at the hospital, she knew all about procedures for blood spillage. But he couldn't help saying it.

'Already seen it,' she reproved him gently and turned towards the medical box. Collecting what he'd asked for, she scooped up the hem of her dress, picking her way carefully across the blood-spattered floor and laying a basin of water and a large wad of gauze down next to him.

'Thanks. I'll need a small bandage in a moment.' Leo set about cleaning as much of the blood off Alan's hand as he could, and then packed the gauze around what was left of his finger. Then he ran out of hands. This was the trouble with medicine outside a hospital or surgery; he always seemed to get to the point when two hands wasn't enough.

'Here, let me.' Alex was there, the hem of her dress gathered in a makeshift knot at the side, to keep it out of the way. She bent over, winding the bandage over the gauze to keep it in place, and secured it with a safety pin.

Leo carefully relaxed his grip on Alan's wrist. Good. He didn't want to use a tourniquet unless absolutely necessary, and it looked as if the bleeding was stopping now.

Alan was quieter now and Leo turned to him, trying

to give a little reassurance. 'You're doing really well. The ambulance will be here soon and we'll get you something for the pain...'

'Where is it?' Alan was looking round, trying to get up now, and Leo pressed him gently backwards. Now that the bleeding was dealt with, he could think about finding the finger. But he needed to stay here with Alan.

And he wasn't quite sure how Alex might react to being asked to find a missing body part. But the one thing he did know was that just assuming she couldn't do it without even mentioning it would hurt her even more.

He smiled at her. 'Tough question. For me to ask, that is...'

She grinned back. 'I know. Easy answer for me...' She laid her gloved hand on the side of Alan's face and his gaze focused on hers. 'Alan, I'm going to find your finger. Can't have you going off to the hospital without it, eh?'

'Please...' Alan tried to move again but she shook her head.

'It's okay. You need to stay here and do what the doctor tells you. I'll find it.'

No one could have resisted the warmth of her smile, the reassuring certainty of her tone. Even Leo felt better. Alan relaxed back against the wall with a small nod, and Alex got to her feet.

'Can you see if you can find something to splint the hand with first?' Alan was still moving fitfully and he should keep his hand as still as possible.

She nodded, opening a couple of drawers and pulling out a flat wooden spatula. 'This do?'

'That's perfect.'

Alex delivered the spatula and another bigger bandage to him and Leo set about immobilising Alan's hand. When he glanced up again, Alex was standing at the counter top, moving the bloodstained knife carefully out of the way and sorting through the pile of peelings and chopped vegetables.

A slight shake of her head told Leo that it wasn't there, and he hoped that it hadn't rolled onto the floor. He'd been watching where he put his feet, but there had obviously been a bit of panic in here when the accident first happened. Alex was obviously thinking the same thing because she stopped, standing still, looking carefully around her.

Then she moved, one step towards the sink, and reached in. 'Got it. It's got some vegetable peelings on it.'

'Okay, get as much as you can off, but don't put it under water. Leave anything that isn't easy to remove for the surgeon at the hospital. Then wrap it with some moist gauze.'

She followed his instructions and then looked in the medical box, breaking open a plastic bag and tipping the contents back into the box. Alex slid the precious gauze-wrapped package into the bag, securing it carefully with some plaster.

'Great. Now the ice, but make sure it's not in contact with any tissue.' Leo decided not to say *finger*. Alan was calmer now and he didn't want to upset him any further.

'Gotcha.' She walked over to the fridge and found a bag of crushed ice. Tearing it open, she tipped half into the sink and then put the package with Alan's finger in it carefully into the bag, packing the ice around it and resealing the top.

She walked back over to them and bent down next to Alan. 'Here, I've got it. It's undamaged and on ice.'

'They'll be able to sew it back on?' Alan reached for the bag and Alex caught his hand, allowing him to touch it but not grab hold of it.

'There's a good chance they will.' She curled her hand over Alan's. 'They'll have to make an assessment, but these days the surgeons can do what seems like the impossible. We've done all the right things, and they'll explain everything to you when you get there.'

It was just the right mix of truth and reassurance. And there was no trace in her manner of the stark truth that the surgeons hadn't been able to do the impossible for her. He'd never met anyone who was quite so generous with hope as Alex was.

'Thank you... What's your name?'

'Alexandra.' The use of her full name seemed just right at this moment. Something beautiful, a reassurance to Alan that even now there was time to appreciate the extra syllables.

'P...pretty name.'

'Thank you.' Alan moved restively and Alex caught hold of the bag a little tighter, steadying it without taking it away from him. 'I know it hurts. The paramedics will be here soon and they'll be able to give you something for the pain.'

Voices and movement at the other side of the kitchen confirmed her statement, almost as if she'd magicked them. A paramedic walked towards them.

'Not much for us to do here, then?' His practised eye took in Alan's bandaged hand and the bag of ice.

Leo supervised the administration of pain relief and Alan was settled into a portable wheelchair. Alex entrusted the bag to the paramedic's care and gave Alan a little wave and a brilliant smile as he was wheeled out.

'How do you do that?' Alex had turned to him.

'Do what?'

'Look at you.' She gazed at his shirt, inspecting it carefully. 'You have one tiny spot on your sleeve, but apart from that you're as clean as a whistle.'

Leo laughed. 'I worked in A&E for a while, when I was training. You get an instinct for avoiding all kinds of spatter.'

'And there was me thinking that you'd picked the knack up from your tailor.' She giggled.

'Nah. He'd be delighted if I went through a few more shirts. Better for business.' Leo stripped off his gloves, throwing them into the bag he'd put to one side for the bloodstained towel and dressings, and Alex followed suit.

He walked over to a sink at the far end of the room, lathering his hands with liquid soap.

Suddenly she was next to him, holding her fingers under the tap. He tipped a little of the soap onto her hand, working it round with his fingers, expecting her to draw away from him at any moment, but she didn't. She just stayed still, her face tilted downwards so that he could only see the top of her head, allowing him to lace his fingers with hers then rub her palms and the back of her hands.

If he'd strayed over the line, made a touch into a caress, Leo felt sure that she would have drawn back. But in his head he was way past practical, heading through sensual at breakneck speed and making for sexual. Before thoughts turned into actions, he reached for the dispenser, putting a paper towel into her hands.

Letting his gaze trace her arms and ankles wasn't sexual either. It was strictly practical. 'You've got a smudge on your leg…there.'

'Oh…my prosthesis…' She leaned over to scrub the dried blood with the paper towel, but her dress seemed to have other ideas, choosing this moment to slip from the knot she'd tied to keep it clear of her ankles. She grappled with it, pulling it away from her legs.

'Here…' Leo put his hands tentatively around her waist and she didn't wriggle free, so he lifted her, perching her up on the counter top. She pulled her dress up, exposing her knees.

'Some soap and water…' She bent down, removing the prosthesis and examining it, the remaining part of her leg covered with a thin white sock and hanging unnoticed.

She'd talked about practically every issue that she faced in front of him, and he'd seen amputees remove a prosthesis many times before. But, watching her now, he was no doctor. He was her date for the evening, someone that she'd dressed up for. It was warming that Alex seemed to trust him on that level too.

'I'll get it…' He pulled one of the towels from the dispenser and dribbled some soap and water into it. She held the prosthesis away from her dress and he wiped the blood away, making sure that there was no mark left on the silicone skin-toned covering.

'That's it… Oops, no, there's some on my shoe.' She unbuckled the pretty silver sandal and examined the dark stain covering the inside of the sole. There was a corresponding smear on the heel of her prosthesis, and Leo wiped that away.

'Rhona's going to kill me.' She was balancing the prosthesis on her lap.

'They're hers?'

Alex nodded. 'Yep. Four ninety-nine from the market. She sprayed them silver…' She ran her nail along the straps and silver paint flaked off onto the floor.

'We'll get her another pair. I think I can spare four ninety-nine.'

'No, we can't. She got them from some stall that does recycled stuff. They're a one-off.'

'We'll think of something. Do you want to go? The evening's probably winding down by now.' And Leo couldn't bear to give her up to the other people in the room. Not now.

'Yes. I'm ready to go now.'

'Okay. Take your other sandal off.'

'Why—is that stained too?' She swung her leg up to inspect her foot.

'No.' Leo leaned in close, planting his hands on the counter on either side of her. 'But there are three public relations options here.'

'As many as that?' The subtle curve of her lips in an otherwise solemn expression told Leo that she was teasing him.

'Yep. If I carry you out of here and into the car—'

'What would you want to do that for?'

'Because if you put your shoe back on you'll stain your

heel. And you can't go barefoot over the gravel in the car park.' She pressed her lips together, nodding. 'So I can carry you out and everyone will think you're a poor thing who can't walk. I don't think we'll go for that option.'

'No.' She grinned. 'I don't think we will.'

'Or…they can think that I'm sweeping you off for a night of passion and I can't keep my hands off you.' At that moment, that sounded pretty much perfect to Leo.

'No. Probably not…'

She was right, of course. 'Or…you hold your stained shoes in your hand, and everyone thinks I'm just carrying you because you can't wear them.'

She nodded. 'Wisest choice, I think.'

'We'll go for that one then. Where's your evening bag?'

'I left it with that terribly important, terribly nice man. His wife's looking after it for me.'

'Right. I'll go and fetch that, and our coats, and make sure they're sending someone up to clean up this mess.' He let his hand stray to her right leg, brushing her knee with his fingers. 'Will you wait for me here? I won't be long.'

She grinned. 'That's fine. I'll yell if I need you.'

Leo made a show of rolling his eyes. She was more than enchanting. And they'd broken through a barrier. Alex's independent streak usually made her cautious about taking help, but she'd let her guard down with him tonight.

He turned away from her, pulling the sleeves of his shirt down and refastening his cufflinks before he put his jacket back on.

'Wait…' She beckoned him back over and she reached up, untying his bow tie and leaving it to drape around his neck, then unbuttoning the top button of his shirt.

'And what's that for?'

'If we're worried about how things look, then I think you should seem a little less neat. You can't battle for someone's life with your tie done up.'

'It's practical. Keeps it out of the way.' He grinned at her.

'Yes, I know, but we're thinking image here.' She reached forward, flipping open the second button on his shirt, and Leo felt a tingle run down his spine. 'That's much better. Makes you look very dashing.'

Leo was back in less than five minutes, accompanied by the hotel's cleaning crew. He *did* look enormously dashing.

He didn't just look the part. He'd saved her from the monstrous blue and black dresses in the ladies' room, and made her feel as if she was beautiful. If he hadn't saved Alan's life, he'd come pretty close to it and sent him off to hospital strong enough to undergo the complex surgery needed to reattach his finger.

He leaned across, gathering her up in his arms. 'You're heavier than you look.'

'Muscle weighs more than fat. You must be weaker than you look.' He was having no trouble carrying her at all. She picked up her sandals from the counter top and curled the other arm around his neck.

'Door…'

She reached down for the door handle, pulling it open, and he manoeuvred through and along the concrete floor of the corridor, setting her back on her feet when they reached the carpeted area in the lobby. Smiling at the group who had gathered in the lobby, ready to go, he caught sight of Justin and shook his hand. A hotel employee was waiting with their coats and her bag and walked towards the entrance doors.

'Leo…' The woman in the blue dress had appeared suddenly from nowhere and was making determinedly for him.

'Clara. Nice to see you. Be a darling and get the door for me, would you.'

Leo swung back to face Alex, grim satisfaction burning in his eyes as he picked her up again. This wasn't one of Leo's charming jokes; he'd meant to put Clara firmly in her place.

Her dress brushed against Clara's arm as he whisked her through the door and out into the night. The cold air made her shiver, and she instinctively clung a little tighter to him.

For once, Leo was tight-lipped and silent, almost as if he'd been hurt by Clara's remarks as much as she had. 'It doesn't matter, Leo. She's not important.'

'Yeah.' He didn't sound all that convinced. 'Car keys. In my pocket.'

She made a bit more of a meal of feeling in his jacket pocket than she strictly needed to, and Leo finally smiled. 'Stop that. Or I'll throw you over my shoulder.'

CHAPTER THIRTEEN

TWENTY MINUTES ON the motorway and then they started to meander along narrow roads, through pretty villages. Then he turned off the road entirely, the car bumping slightly on a muddy track. To the left of them, the moon reflected in a long, shimmering trail across a stretch of dark water.

'Oh, look, Leo. Is it a full moon?'

'Tomorrow, I think.'

'Your house is near here?' She couldn't see any buildings ahead of them, just fields.

'Over there.' He pointed across the water and Alex saw the shadow of a house, nestling amongst the trees, overlooking the millpond. There must be a bridge up ahead of them.

But he slowed the car, backing it onto an area of hard-standing which was surrounded on three sides by stone-built walls and covered over by a small pitched roof. He got out, walking to the back of the parking space, and suddenly she was in wonderland.

Lights led all the way to the building. Along a paved path to a bridge, which stretched across the mouth of the stream that fed into the millpond. Across the bridge and then up a sharp incline, with steps set into it, to the front door of a solid two-storey timber-framed house.

The only way to get there was to walk. Alex had her trainers packed in her bag, ready for tomorrow, along with her sports leg. But suddenly the idea of being carried across, snuggling in Leo's arms as the night breeze caught her dress, seemed unbearably tempting.

He walked around the car, opening her door. 'You can walk, can't you?'

'Yes. I just need my trainers from my bag.'

He nodded. Without a word, he lifted her out of the car, settling her in his arms. She curled her arm around his neck, feeling his warmth.

'This is lovely. It's all yours?'

'I own the land but there's a public footpath which runs from the road, along this side of the millpond and through to the village. It's a bit of a tradition that people come and fish here during the summer and I wouldn't want that to change.'

'That's nice. A hideaway with plenty of people passing back and forth on the other side of the water.'

'Yeah. That's what I like about it. I lent the place to Evie for a couple of weeks last summer, and when the paparazzi stopped at the village pub and asked how to get here, they pointed them thirty miles in the other direction.' He chuckled quietly.

'Did they ever find her?'

'No.' He stopped halfway across the bridge, turning so she could see across the millpond. 'This is one of my favourite spots.'

'It's beautiful.' The water stretched out in front of them, moving gently. There were trees and a clear, dark sky, studded with stars. It was like being in the arms of a handsome prince, who was carrying her across a gilded lake to his castle.

Leo climbed the steps to the front porch, setting her down for a moment while he opened the door and flipped the light on. When she stepped inside, the hallway was bright and warm.

'Make yourself at home. I'll go and get the coats and bags and lock the car...' He left her alone in the hallway.

Her prosthetic foot was angled slightly to accommodate the heel of a shoe, and Alex had to walk on her toes. It somehow felt right to be tiptoeing through Leo's house, exploring it, like a lost princess. The kitchen was straight ahead, modern and utilitarian, much as she would have expected. But the sitting room came as a revelation. A stone fireplace, obviously used, from the pile of wood in the hearth. Large squashy sofas in powder blue and oak cabinets, full of books and ornaments which looked like an eclectic collection, made over the years.

The dining room was just as welcoming, wood-framed French windows with patterned curtains and a distressed wooden table. It was stylish but it felt like a home, and it was light years away from his London flat.

She heard him in the hallway and went back out to meet him. 'So it's your alter ego who lives here?'

'Not really. I'm the same person here as I am in London.'

It was another piece in the puzzle. Just as Leo's secrets had filled in the blanks, made sense of a complex and seemingly disjointed personality, this house did too. There was the Leo who loved the bright lights and the excitement of London, but that Leo needed a home and this was it.

He took her bag upstairs, showing her to a comfortable, elegant room with French windows opening onto a balcony and an en suite bathroom. It was clearly appropriate that he should make cocoa, since it seemed cocktails were reserved for the London flat. He took off his jacket, sitting down on one of the sofas while Alex curled up on the other.

'I'm really sorry about tonight.' A shadow passed across his brow. 'Didn't really go to plan, did it?'

'I suppose not. But what were you going to do—let the man bleed to death?'

'No. But if he *had* to chop his finger off, I wish he'd done it some other time. This Saturday was intended to make up for rushing off last Saturday.' His phone was on the arm of the chair and he was turning it over and over restlessly.

'You don't have to make anything up to me, Leo. Is life usually so eventful with you, though?'

He laughed, shaking his head. 'No. I seem to be having a busy period at the moment. Usually, I can go for weeks on end without people keeling over in my vicinity.'

'That's good to hear. I was beginning to worry that I might be next.'

'You won't be.' A pulse beat suddenly at the side of his brow, as if he was going to prevent anything from happening to her by the sheer force of his will.

'I know. I was just joking.'

'Yeah. I wasn't.'

How could she explain to him? She'd been proud to be part of the difference that Leo had made tonight. And somehow, when they were working together with a shared aim, it felt as if their connection was strongest. Work was his way of forgetting the incessant tug of the past, and living only in the present.

She drained the last few mouthfuls of cocoa from her mug. Leo was the best man she'd ever met. And the one she could never have because his attention would always be somewhere else.

'It's late. I should go to bed.' There was nothing more that she could say.

'Yes. I'll be turning in soon. Sleep well.' He reached for the slim leather laptop case that he'd brought in with the bags, and left on the coffee table.

If it wasn't a patient, it was his phone. And if it wasn't his phone, it was emails to read or papers to review. Leo just couldn't switch off.

'Hasn't your battery run down yet?' Alex suppressed the urge to snatch the laptop from him and pour the rest of his cocoa into the keyboard.

His lips twitched into a smile. 'I always carry a spare.'

'Too bad. Goodnight.' As she walked up the stairs, she heard a quiet tone from the sitting room as his laptop booted up. However late it was, it seemed there was always one more thing that couldn't wait until the morning.

Alex always knew when she was in the country as soon as she woke up. Even with the windows tightly closed against the chill of the morning outside, she could still hear the faint chirrup of birds, and still smell the clean scents that reminded her of home.

She'd left the curtains open, knowing that she'd wake with the dawn. As light began to filter through the windows, she rolled to the edge of the bed.

This was the time in the day when she felt loss. A new day, new challenges, the sun rising outside her window. But, instead of rising to meet it, she had either to crawl or do as she was doing now, lean down to reach the collapsible crutches that were stowed in her travel bag and snap them into rigid supports. Soon enough, she'd go through the morning ritual of rubbing cream into her residual limb, checking it for any skin abrasions or blisters and pulling on the thin fabric sock which acted as a liner for her prosthesis.

But, for now, there was something missing. She couldn't tumble straight out of bed to face the bright morning that was outside her window without pausing for a moment.

It was a small thing. At first, she'd mourned her leg in the same way that she would have mourned a death. But that had eased, and if each new day brought a moment of remembrance then perhaps that was what it was supposed to do. A moment when she could remember how things were and how she'd turned that around.

She swung her body between the crutches, over to the window. The shadows she'd seen outside last night were now a deep balcony, big enough to sit on and have breakfast in the summer. When she craned round she could see that it ran along the whole of the back of the house, and that there were doors leading onto it further down. Leo's bedroom, maybe.

She could imagine him walking along the balcony to tap on her window. Climbing up with a rose between his teeth. Alex grinned at the thought. Maybe not between his teeth—that was a little makeshift for Leo. It would have to be his buttonhole.

And on summer mornings maybe he sat out here, watching the sun rise. Coffee and orange juice, alone with the sounds of the countryside.

She stared at the frost-sprinkled fields on the horizon, allowing the balcony to drop into soft focus. Morning was the time when loss might be touched and then left behind. But she couldn't touch Leo and then leave *him* behind.

The view from her window would still be here when she was washed and dressed. Alex made her way into the shining, white-tiled bathroom and opened the door of the shower enclosure, ready to contemplate her next move.

A non-slip mat. Good. A couple of grab rails. Not all that common in a private house, but even better. She leaned forward to test the rigidity of one of them, finding it firm and in exactly the right place. Then a little sprinkle of dust fell from it, red on the white tiles.

She leaned down to inspect it. Brick dust. The grab rail was solid and secure enough, though…

These were new. They were for her.

It wasn't what he'd done, but the motive behind it. Leo had never shown any doubt as to her independence. This was his practical version of chocolates on her pillow. Freshly squeezed orange juice in the morning, or thick towels left on her bed. He'd taken the time to come down here and install a pair of grab rails. They didn't have red ribbons tied around them but it was the sweetest thing he could have done.

* * *

Leo had hoped that working until his head swam with exhaustion would guarantee unbroken sleep when he finally did go to bed. But still he woke in the night, aware of Alex's silent presence in the house.

He couldn't allow himself to contemplate the short walk along the balcony, the idea of tapping on the glass and finding Alex awake and waiting for him. It might be below zero out there but he had a feeling that being packed in ice couldn't cool the heat which seemed to draw him to her.

Breakfast was easier because he had something to do, to divert his attention from her smile. And this morning she *was* smiling, obviously enjoying the bright morning as much as he was.

'Ready to go?' Alex's holdall was in the hall, the ruined silver sandals in a plastic bag on top of it. She was dressed in a warm fleece top and leggings, her hair scrunched into a ponytail. The one delicious reminder of last night was the delicate shine of clear polish on her fingernails.

'Yes. You've got the coordinates?' Alex had given him a set of coordinates instead of a postcode to enter into the satnav. Clearly, her father's farm was relatively remote.

'Yep.' Leo decided that asking whether he could carry her over the bridge to the car was one step too far in wanting to recreate last night.

The morning was cold and crisp, seeming to hold all the potential of a new day. As he drove, the busy patchwork of villages and towns gave way to the more open landscape of the countryside.

'Is this right?' They'd reached the brow of a hill and, in the clear morning, he could see a smudge on the horizon which looked like the sea. In between there were just fields, dotted with clumps of trees and criss-crossed by narrow roads.

'Yep. Turn off right there.' She pointed to a track which

wound around the edge of a field, leading to a large brick-built barn.

'You climb in a barn?'

'It's been converted. Wait till you get there.' There was a hint of pride in her voice which told Leo that the barn had been subjected to Alex's endless ingenuity and energy. This he had to see.

As they drew nearer, he could see a battered truck parked outside. He stopped next to it on the hardstanding area and Alex jumped out of the car, obviously eager to show him inside.

Two sets of doors acted as an air lock. It was still chilly inside the barn but a good few degrees warmer than outside.

'Dad…' Alex ran over to a man who was sweeping the floor, greeting him with a hug. 'This is Leo.'

Leo stepped forward, taking the man's outstretched hand. Although his hair was salt-and-pepper grey, he had the same thoughtful brown eyes as Alex.

'Howard Jackson. I've been listening to the programmes that Alex has been doing with you. I'm delighted to get the chance to meet you.'

A little shiver of embarrassment hit Leo. It felt as if he and Alex had been carrying out a very public exercise in intimacy over the last three weeks, and that had been okay up till now. Better than okay—it had made callers feel at ease and allowed everyone to talk freely. But at this moment it felt as if he needed to apologise for it.

'We've been… Alex has been great. She's a natural…'

'Nice of you to say so.' Howard smiled at his daughter. *His* daughter. 'I detected a fair bit of guidance on your part.'

'More than a bit, Dad. Leo's taught me a lot.'

'It's just a matter of…' Leo shrugged. This wasn't just an exercise in seeing who could compliment who the most; it was suddenly important. 'Alex gave us a lot of direction about what issues to cover. We helped her present them in a way she was comfortable with.'

Howard chuckled, apparently unfazed by the idea of his daughter discussing sex, thinly disguised as body issues, on the radio. 'I like to call it *direction* as well. Even if she doesn't compromise about exactly which direction she's going in.'

Alex rolled her eyes, nudging her father in the ribs. 'Where's Mum?'

'She's descaling the urn. Should be finished by now; I was just about to go and collect her.' Howard pulled a bunch of keys from his pocket and Alex took them from him.

'I'll go. You can show Leo around.'

And then she was gone, in a flurry of smiles and activity, leaving Leo standing alone with Howard. Somehow he got the impression that this had been some kind of plan.

Leo looked around the space, aware that Howard's gaze was on him. The whole of one side comprised a set of climbing walls, ranging from very easy to what looked like pretty difficult. There was a play area for younger children and thick crash mats were stacked in the corner, ready to transform the area into a safe space where kids could try things out without fear of hurting themselves.

'This is impressive. How often do you use this place?'

'Only a couple of times a month in the winter, because of the cost of heating it. We put in a false ceiling, and partitioned the space to make it viable. This area's about a third of the internal floor area.'

'It's a good size, though. And it's warm enough in here.'

'Yes, we have infrared heaters and they take the chill off. Once we get twenty or thirty people in here it's fine for activities. And in the summer we can take the dividing partition down and do more.'

'What kind of things?' This was obviously very well thought out.

'There's a riding stable close by, and they come and do lessons from time to time. We have a picnic area, and Alex organises family days and different activities. She's even got an eye on laying a proper running surface, but that's all pie in the sky at the moment.'

'At the moment…' Leo grinned. That sounded expensive but, if he knew anything about Alex, it wouldn't be pie in the sky for too much longer. She'd find a way.

Howard chuckled. 'Yes.'

'Do you get many down from London? It's a fair drive.'

'Two, maybe three cars full; the London parents take turns with the driving. There's local demand as well, and we never have any spare places for our activities. Safety considerations limit how many people we can have here at once.'

'This must all have taken a while.'

'Nine years.' Howard stuffed his hands into the pockets of his jacket, looking around as if suddenly he couldn't quite believe they'd done it all. 'We started small. The barn was on some extra land that I'd bought, and surplus to requirements. Alex's brothers and I built her the first climbing wall, in the summer after she lost her leg.'

A lump formed in Leo's throat. 'So this is where it all started?'

'Yes. The number of times I saw her fall off that damn thing, and then get right back up and try again…' Howard shrugged. 'I don't know where she gets it from. Her mother, probably.'

Leo doubted that was entirely true. He could see the same tough determination in Howard as he saw in Alex, and he couldn't help liking him. Which made him feel like a fraud for hiding the way he'd failed Alex from her father.

'I… I met Alex a while ago. At a party.'

'Yes, she told me. Some fancy dress thing…'

'Yes. It was actually the night before she had her accident.' This was turning into a confession but it was one he should make. 'We spent the night…just talking.'

Howard laughed. 'Alex always did have a lot to say for herself.'

'I meant…' He felt like a teenager, telling his date's father that he respected her and that he wouldn't dream of doing anything more than holding her hand.

'I know what you meant. I'm her father, not her gate-keeper. Alex made that very clear to me from a very early age.' Howard turned as if that was an end to it.

'I walked her to the bus stop in the morning. I didn't take her all the way home… I'm sorry.'

Howard nodded, facing him quietly. 'Do you know what *I* did? Alex used to call us every Sunday morning. I was busy on the farm and when she didn't call that day, I didn't think anything of it. When my wife got the call from the hospital, she had to run across the fields to find me.'

Leo stared at him. There were no words, but Howard seemed to be able to find some.

'When Alex was born, her mother put her into my arms and I counted her fingers and toes. Then I promised her that I'd always keep her safe.' Howard leaned towards him. 'You only found out about the accident recently?'

'I called her that day, but she didn't answer. I thought she…' Leo shrugged. 'You know. You call, and they've thought better of it and don't answer.'

Howard chuckled. 'Yeah. I've been there a few times too. Look, you can't blame yourself for something like this. Give it time.'

Leo wasn't convinced of that. But somehow it was as if Alex had spoken to him. He wondered whether she'd put him alone with her father for exactly the same reason that she'd put Carys's father with the other parents. He wouldn't put it past her.

'Thank you.'

'Don't thank me.' Howard seemed just as aware of their places in Alex's master plan as he was. 'But you can come and give me a hand with those crash mats…'

CHAPTER FOURTEEN

IT HAD TAKEN a couple of hours' work before the space was ready, but the transformation was complete. There was enough time for soup and sandwiches at noon, before the first cars started to arrive.

He recognised some of the people. Hayley was there with Alice, and Sam broke free from his mother's hand, tugging at Leo's jacket to tell him that today they were going to climb. Carys's father hovered by the doorway and Howard marched up to him, shaking his hand and taking him and Carys on a guided tour of all the facilities that the barn had to offer. Alex was busy, making sure she spoke to everyone and that the helpers were all in place before anyone started to climb.

At three o'clock refreshments were served, and Alex brought him coffee. 'Enjoying yourself?'

'You need an answer to that?'

She grinned up at him. 'Nah. I saw you at the wall with Sam. He doesn't give up, does he?'

'Incorrigible. Like someone else I know.'

'Can't think who you mean.' She looked around to make sure they weren't being overheard. 'The last of the trustees called me just now, so I can finish the paperwork on Alice's grant in the morning. I've asked her mother if I can pop in for a chat tomorrow, before the radio show.'

'That's great. Thanks.' Leo knew what Alex was asking.

'I don't suppose you want to change your mind and come along with me?'

'No. I don't suppose I do. This is your forte. I prefer to stay at arm's length.'

She shot him an incredulous look. 'How can you say that? You connect with people all the time, as a doctor and on the radio.'

'That's different.'

Alex flushed pink. That was generally a sign that she wasn't going to accept his stonewalling tactics. 'So it's okay to commit emotionally to people you don't know, but not to people you do…' She pressed her lips together. Perhaps she'd said more than she meant to.

He should walk away. Before they got onto why he couldn't commit to her. Because he had a feeling that this was where this was leading. 'Hey. Do me a favour, will you?'

'Of course.'

'Give me a break?'

She laughed suddenly, shaking her head. Maybe she was as relieved as he was to just steer away from a question that ultimately didn't have any answer. 'Yeah. Always.'

'Thanks.'

'Anyway, I think someone's got a job for you.' She pointed over to the most difficult climbing wall and he saw Sam standing at the bottom of it, gazing fixedly in his direction.

'He has *got* to be kidding…'

'I don't think he is. Go and use that charm of yours to talk him out of it.'

The last words that Leo said on-air to her were the ones that mattered the most to him. The ones he really meant. There had been so many callers that they'd been almost overwhelmed and hardly had time for anything else. But he made sure there was time for this.

'This last month has been both inspiring and life-changing for me. It's been an honour to make that journey with you, Alex.'

'Thanks, Leo. I've really enjoyed it.'

'We must do this again, soon.' He held her gaze, trying to show her that this wasn't just a hollow courtesy.

'I'd love to.' He thought he saw the glint of a tear in her eye, and he turned to a commercial before anyone noticed the lump in his throat.

She watched him silently as he took off his headphones and switched off the sound link to the control room. Then she puffed out a breath.

'So this is it...'

'I never say anything I don't mean on the radio.'

'Too many witnesses?'

Leo shook his head. 'Nah. It's just too important to me.'

She gave him a hesitant smile. 'You could...call me. I promise I'll get back to you this time.'

That was all he wanted to hear. 'I know where you live now. If you don't get back to me I *will* find you.'

'That's it.' Rhona put the last of the thank you letters into an envelope and added it to the pile. 'How are you doing with the cheques?'

'They're all ready for the bank.' It had taken all morning and half the afternoon to deal with all the letters and cheques that had been received in the post since last week. Alex was grateful for every word, every penny, but it presented a whole new set of challenges for the charity.

'Growing pains...' Rhona rested her chin on her hand, staring across the desks.

'Yeah. It's going to be a lot of work, spending all this money wisely.' Alex traced the tip of her pencil across her writing pad.

'I blame Leo. And you, of course.'

'Thanks. Nice to know I'm the architect of my own difficulties.' She stared at the complex doodle in front of her. Boxes in boxes in boxes. That was how she'd felt for the last week. She'd known that Leo wouldn't be in touch until after the weekend; he'd been busy filming for a TV special. And today he'd be at his surgery and then the radio station for his Monday evening show. Maybe she could start hoping for a call tomorrow evening.

'We'll work it out.' Alex added a couple of optimistic curlicues to the doodle and then jumped as a loud rap sounded on the door and it swung open.

Leo. The tip of Alex's pencil broke, lead spinning across the desk. Instead of breezing in, the way he normally did, he was standing stock-still in the doorway. And he was smiling.

'Anyone for cake?' He had a box from the cake shop around the corner balanced on top of three takeaway cups in a cardboard holder.

'Leo! Don't be ridiculous—of course we want cake.' Rhona pulled him into the office, slamming the door behind him to prevent any possibility of escape.

He grinned, and Alex's heart lurched dangerously. Had he somehow become more handsome in the last week, or had she really missed him that much?

'Sit down.' Rhona pushed a chair up for him and grabbed the box from his hand, opening it. 'Ah, Leo. You know the way to a woman's heart…'

He chuckled, putting a cardboard cup down in front of her and a second on Rhona's desk, keeping the smaller cup for himself.

'Espresso?' It was all Alex could think of to say. Still she couldn't stop staring at him, but that was okay because his gaze had never left her face.

'Yeah. I need to stay awake. I've been busy.'

He probably had been. But *busy* was Leo's excuse for everything. All the same, he was here, and all the reasons why she shouldn't miss him were crushed under the weight of his smile.

'I'm just off to the bank. Don't eat my cake...' Rhona snatched up the pile of cheques from Alex's desk.

'It's my turn.' Alex shot her an apologetic look. She supposed that she and Leo had made Rhona feel as if she was the third person who made up a crowd. 'I'll go later.'

'I don't mind. You and Leo stay here...'

'Actually...' Leo put a stop to the discussion. 'I have something I wanted to discuss with you both. What are you doing on Saturday?'

Alex looked at her watch. Twelve thirty, and the barn was already filling up. They'd decided to use the larger area because of the number of people coming today, and she had taken the previous day off work to help clear the space. Early this morning, a group of men had turned up with a van and erected a stage, messed around with amplifiers and microphones until everything was exactly to their liking and then left again. And now nothing seemed to be happening.

'Where is he? Suppose they don't turn up?' she whispered frantically to Rhona.

'You said it yourself—Leo's never early. We've got another half an hour.'

'Yes, but...' They'd brought all of these people down here on the promise of an unspecified music performance, after Leo had pointed out that making what they were planning public was likely to bring an influx of outsiders that they couldn't cope with. They had a sound stage and equipment, but there had been no word from Leo.

She pulled out her phone and looked at it. Nothing. And it was impossible that Leo didn't have his phone with him. He'd call if there was a problem.

'You just want to see him,' Rhona observed sagely.

'No…' Yes, actually. 'At the moment I'd just like to see someone on that stage…'

Suddenly the door at the far end of the barn, next to the stage, opened. Her father ushered Leo through it and Alex's heart thumped in her chest. Then a young man walked through the door, climbing up onto the stage.

Bobby Carusoe. The name was passed around the scattered audience like a brush fire. Six number one hits in a row. The young star who had taken both America and Europe by storm and who was in the UK for six weeks between tours. Every teenage girl's dream.

Every head turned towards him, mouths gaping open. Bobby picked up a microphone and addressed the stunned crowd.

'Is everyone here yet?'

'No…' Rhona shouted at the top of her voice, from where she and Alex were standing at the back. 'It's supposed to start at one o'clock…'

'Then there's time to meet everyone.' A communal gasp went up. 'But first I'd like you all to meet a good friend of mine.'

'Friend?' Alex hissed at Rhona, 'What's he done now? Leo didn't say anything about a friend.'

'Oh, my giddy aunt…' Rhona nodded towards the stage, where Leo was helping a young woman in high heels and a shimmering dress up the steps. She ran towards Bobby, smiling up at him when he put his arm around her shoulder. 'It's Aleesha.'

Bobby and Aleesha waved and everyone waved back. Then Aleesha put her finger to her lips, and everyone fell silent.

'Bobby and I have a new album, due to come out next week. And we thought you might like to be the first to hear some of the songs.'

A deafening *'Yes!'* sounded through the barn, and Alex nudged Rhona in the ribs.

'I didn't know that. What on earth are they going to sing together?' Bobby was known for his soulful love songs, but Aleesha's style was more upbeat. It didn't seem as if they had an awful lot in common.

'Who cares? They're here, aren't they?'

Bobby jumped down from the stage and lifted his arms to swing Aleesha down next to him. Alex moved forward, afraid that there might be a crush around them, but Leo was there with another man and the carefully calculated child to helper ratio meant that everyone kept relatively calm. Bobby and Aleesha split up, obviously intent on getting to speak to everyone, however briefly.

Alex was trembling. She'd been unsure about Leo's idea at first, knowing that it might be difficult to control a barn full of teenagers in the presence of a pop idol. But they'd talked it through and Leo had answered all of her questions. Bobby's people would be instructed to stay back, and treat the kids with care and respect, and there would be enough adults there to make sure that there was no risk of injury to anyone. And he'd been right. Although everyone was excited, the event was well under control.

Leo was making his way over to her, stopping briefly to exchange a few words with some of the teenagers and their parents. The thought that Bobby and Aleesha were here, in her dad's barn, and that they were going to sing, paled into insignificance. Leo was here, and he was making straight for her.

'You made it.' She smiled up at him.

'Always do.' He grinned back.

'What are they going to sing? I can't imagine that they'd find anything that they both liked, let alone could sing together.'

'The new album's all oldies. Some rock and roll, a few ballads, done in their own way. It's interesting.'

'You've heard it?'

'They played it in the car on the way down.'

'How did you swing this, Leo? Bobby *and* Aleesha?'

'I told you. Friend of a friend. And, anyway, they're pretty much inseparable.'

'They're...going out?'

Leo nodded. 'Yep. For about a year now, only it's been a big secret. This album's a big risk for both of them; not only are they trying out some different kinds of music but they're going to go public with the fans. How many more people are you expecting?'

'Well, we've got forty kids and the same number of parents and helpers now. I reckon about another twenty of each.'

Leo nodded. 'Sounds good.' His fingers brushed the back of her hand. Then again, lingering a little longer this time. She took his arm, smiling up at him.

'Anyone remember this?' Bobby sang a couple of chords and Aleesha nodded and joined in.

'I do...' Alex's father shouted from the side of the stage.

'Help us out with the words, then.' Aleesha grinned down at him, and he laughed.

The two of them were just perfect. Keeping everyone under control so that parents and helpers were able to stand back and enjoy the performance too. The chemistry between them was obvious, and they talked with the audience almost as much as they sang.

'Dad loves this one. He used to sing it to us when we were kids.'

Her father was singing now and Aleesha walked over to him, bending down to share her microphone for a couple of bars. Bobby's hand went to his heart in an exaggerated expression of loss and then he beckoned Aleesha back and she strutted across the stage, into his arms.

'Never mind, Howard...' one of the helpers shouted above the music, and her father laughed uproariously.

'Glad you did this?' Leo leaned towards her.

'Yes. It was a risk, but… Yes, I'm so glad we did it.' She moved a little closer to him and felt his arm light around her shoulder. Then tighter, more possessive. That was another risk, but one that suddenly seemed worth taking.

Bobby and Aleesha stayed for three hours, far beyond what anyone expected, singing, talking to everyone and posing for photographs. Alex tried to think of words to thank them enough and failed, but they both seemed to get the message. Then they were whisked away in a convoy of three black SUVs.

It was the tidiest concert crowd that Alex had ever seen. Bags were filled with rubbish and taken away. Chairs were folded and stacked neatly and the floor was swept. Alice's mother even attempted to clean the sound stage before Leo bounded up the steps and coaxed her away from the electrical equipment.

'Home?' Leo murmured the word as Alex waved the last of the cars off.

'Yes. Which one?'

He chuckled. 'Any one you like. Lady's privilege.'

She had her overnight things with her, after staying with her parents last night, and they could go anywhere. 'The country, maybe?'

'Give me your car keys. I'll programme your satnav.'

CHAPTER FIFTEEN

SHE LOST LEO behind a large truck, blocking the road through one of the villages. It was dark by the time she swung off the road and onto the track which led to his house, and Alex manoeuvred onto the hardstanding and found the switch for the lights.

He'd dropped his front door key in her hand before climbing into his own car, and all she had to do was follow the trail of lights. Alex hauled her bag out of the boot, carrying it across the bridge and dumping it in the front hall.

She could see headlights, coming towards her along the track. It could only be Leo, and he must see the lights on the bridge ahead of him by now. Pulling the front door to behind her, she walked down the steps and onto the bridge.

His car swung onto the hardstanding next to hers and the headlights almost blinded her. When he switched them off the darkness seemed deeper, and then he came striding out of the gloom towards her.

'Is this a metaphor?' His hands rested lightly on her waist, his lips just an inch away from hers.

'Now you mention it… Maybe.' It had just seemed appropriate to meet him here. Suspended above the water, each reaching out for the other, unsure whether this was anything but a brief moment in the darkness. But, however brief, it was worth any amount of risk.

'I haven't been with anyone in a while.' He seemed

to want her to know that what the papers said about him wasn't true and that this was something special. Leo was finally allowing someone to touch him.

Alex reached up, tracing her fingers across the side of his face. 'I'd be happy to help you out with anything you're unsure of…'

Leo grinned. 'I said it's been a while. I still know what to do.'

Then he kissed her, his lips warm and very tender. She wrapped her arms around his neck, pulling him close. Something wild broke through the last vestiges of doubt and then there was only Leo, his body hard against hers in the cold evening air.

He pulled the zip of her jacket in a movement that was urgent, almost wild. His hand found her breast and, even though there were layers of clothing between them, she imagined she could feel his touch. Alex heard her own whimper of longing, smothered by his kiss.

'I want you *now*…' She nipped at the lobe of his ear and felt his body jolt, like an engine being jerked from first gear straight into overdrive.

'I want you every place and every way.' He backed against the stone parapet, lifting her against him. For one delicious moment she thought that *this* place and *this* way was going to be the start of it all, however unlikely and impractical. Wrapping one arm around his neck, she found the fastening of his jeans with her other hand.

'Forget the metaphor, Alex. It's far too cold. And uncomfortable.'

'I don't want comfort. I don't want pretty words.' She wanted him. Not his practised charm, which would leave her smiling but unchanged. She wanted that raw edge, the one that would respond only to need and be satisfied only with taking everything.

'Hold on tight, then.' He settled her weight against his and she wrapped her legs around his hips. Striding across the bridge, he climbed the steps to the front door, kicking it closed behind him.

He paused in the hallway and she felt him reach into his pocket. Then he put something on the hallstand. 'I'll leave this here…'

She twisted round to look. It was his phone. Alex kissed him, and he suddenly seemed to lose interest in who might or might not be calling him and started to stride up the stairs.

She caught the frame of his bedroom doorway with one hand as they passed through it, jerking them to a halt. 'Lights, Leo.'

'Yeah…' He slammed one hand against the wall and she squeezed her eyes closed as the bedroom was bathed in bright light. Felt him move, and then tip her backwards. Her hands instinctively clutched tighter around his shoulders as she felt herself falling with him onto the bed.

'Open them…' She felt his lips brush her closed eyelids. 'Open your eyes.'

It was almost a command—that she see him, and he see her. Nothing hidden. She blinked and Leo's smile snapped into focus for one brief moment, before he kissed her again.

Her whole body was trembling, aching for him, and it seemed like a criminal act to break the spontaneity. But facts were facts and Leo would find a way to make things all right. 'My bag, Leo…' She felt her lips twist into a grimace. 'I need my crutch, for the bathroom.'

The sweet touch of his hands never faltered. The melting blue of his eyes suddenly made her want to cry.

'If that's what you want, I'll get it.' His fingers found the side of her face, caressing gently. 'Whatever you need, Alex. But I don't need to smell soap when I have your scent. And what's mine is yours. We can manage.'

We can manage. Tonight was all about what they could do together, not whether she could do anything on her own.

'I guess… Three legs is enough for anyone.'

'Yeah. Three legs, four arms…'

'Four eyes, eight fingers.' She used one of those fingers to caress his lips. 'One of me, and one of you…'

'*That*, I'm planning on changing.' He sat up on the bed, drawing her along with him, holding her close. 'Very soon.'

The rhythm didn't break. Urgent, and yet there was time to trade kisses along the way. It never faltered, not when he unbuttoned her shirt, or when she unbuttoned his. Not when she took off her prosthesis, or when he reached for the condoms in the drawer beside the bed.

'Hold me…please…' His eyes were dark and, stretched out under him, she could feel his erection nudging against her. Waiting. Drawing out this last moment until it was a confection of feverish anticipation.

She wrapped her arms around his neck and he reached down. They gasped together as he slid inside. Just a little way.

'Please, Alex…' His fingers gripped her right thigh, then traced down to her knee. Without thinking, she'd kept her right leg away from his back, not sure how he'd react to feeling her foreshortened limb against him, but now she curled both legs around his hips, holding him tight, pulling him further inside.

They both cried out together. Staring into each other's eyes, breathing hard. Tilting her hips, she pushed against him, feeling him slide deeper.

One moment of stillness, to sink into his gaze, and then Leo moved. His gasp was more than pleasure. It was triumph and need, helplessness and mastery.

'Are you going to make me wait, Leo?'

'No, honey. We've waited long enough.' He started to move and the trembling excitement turned into a roar. She didn't have to reach for the orgasm—it was just there, building inside until she came in his arms.

'Again?' He kissed her neck, and she shivered at the touch of his lips against her skin.

'*Again?*'

He changed position slightly, angling his hips to set off a shower of new sensations. 'Again.'

After she'd come the second time, her body straining against his so hard that Leo had almost lost himself, she'd rolled him over onto his back and climbed on top of him. His sweet Alexandra. Taking him until all he knew was that he'd surrendered to her completely, and all he wanted to do was to shout her name out loud.

Perhaps he had. He thought he might have done, but then she'd pushed him further than he'd ever been before. She was strong and athletic, and yet soft at the same time, and when she pinned him down he could watch each movement of her body. Feel each corresponding sensation.

He didn't even properly remember what the orgasm had felt like. Just that he was being pulled into it by an overwhelming force. And that by the time she was done with him all he could do was to curl up with her on the bed, still craving her touch, but more content than he'd thought he ever could be.

They'd slept a little, and then talked a little. Then Leo had gone downstairs to fetch a bottle of champagne. Just the right thing at the right time. Leo, who charmed his way through every situation so adroitly. Only at the moment he seemed deliciously clumsy, spilling half the contents of his glass on the pillow when he pulled her close again to kiss her. And, when he ran a bath, climbing into the hot, foaming water with her, half of it slopped all over the floor and he had to get out and mop the mess up.

Even that was bliss. Lying back in the water, watching his strong body. Each flex of muscle, every square inch of perfect flesh, was capable of giving pleasure. And he was all hers for the night.

And she was his. When the sun rose, he caught her up

from the bed, carrying her over to the window, and they watched the flaming sky together. Then breakfast in bed, tangled in each other's arms. And then they made love again. Lazy, sensual, not driven by the urgency of last night, but time enough to explore each sensation together.

When Leo opened his eyes, the sun was high in the sky and Alex was still sleeping. He watched her for a while, wondering vaguely what time it was. It didn't matter. There was nothing that he could think of to do today, except share it with her.

A quiet beep sounded from downstairs. Must be her phone. Only...

His phone wasn't on the nightstand, where it usually lay. Suddenly he was on the move. Rolling out of bed, grabbing his underwear and running down the stairs. When he'd left his phone downstairs he'd reckoned on retrieving it later in the evening but, wrapped in the warmth of their lovemaking, he'd forgotten all about it.

He picked it up, letting out a sharp curse. Three messages, two missed calls. He scrolled through the messages. Justin's could wait. Evie had texted to say that she and Arielle were leaving London for a few days and they'd catch him when they got back. And there was one from Aleesha, saying that she and Bobby had enjoyed their day yesterday and that they'd have to do it all again some time.

He smiled, walking into the kitchen as he flipped over to the missed calls. Two from his mother. Suddenly the past reared up and smacked him in the face and his hand shook as he pressed the icon to return the call.

'Come on... Come on.' The call switched to voicemail and he ended it. No, he didn't want to leave a message.

He called again and this time his mother answered.

'Mum... Everything okay?' He heard the tremor in his voice.

'Yes, of course it is, darling. I was just calling to remind you about dinner on Tuesday. With Carl and Peter.'

'Oh…yeah. I've got it in my diary. Thanks, Mum.'

'Leo. Whatever's the matter?'

There was seldom any way of fooling her acute radar when it came to her son.

'Nothing…' That wasn't going to wash. She'd only start worrying about him. 'I had a long day yesterday, and I didn't sleep much last night. I've only just got up and there are a load of messages on my phone.'

'Oh, for goodness' sake, Leo. It's Sunday. They can wait, can't they?'

'Yeah. Okay, Mum. Look, I'm standing in my underwear in the kitchen.'

'That I *didn't* want to know. Go and put some clothes on.'

'Okay. See you on Tuesday evening, then. About seven-ish?'

'That'll be fine. And don't bring any wine this time; your father's just gone out and bought two cases, and he's left them in the kitchen for me to trip over. My only hope of getting them out of the way is to drink as much of it as we can.'

Leo ended the call and put the phone down on the counter top. There was nothing to worry about. Everything was okay, so why did it still feel as if his heart was trying to pound its way through his ribcage?

He knew why. He'd finally let go with Alex. Forgotten about everything else and surrendered himself completely to her. It made no difference that the fears which had propelled him downstairs this morning had been unfounded. His guilt was that of a watchman who had deserted his post.

A bump from upstairs disturbed his reverie. Now what? He took the stairs two at a time and when he reached the bedroom he found Alex sitting on the bed, wrapped in his dressing gown and rubbing her knee.

'Are you okay?'

She tipped her head up towards him, smiling through the tears in her eyes. 'Yes, I'm fine. Just took a tumble.'

She must have got out of bed when he was downstairs. He'd made sure to pick up their discarded clothes from the floor when he'd got up yesterday evening and, without thinking, he'd moved her prosthetic leg away from the bedside and into the corner, where they couldn't trip over it.

'Did you hurt yourself?'

'No. You have nice thick carpet.'

Leo suddenly realised that she was looking at the phone in his hand. In his panic, he'd broken his promise to her. *We can manage.* He'd put all the things that kept her independent out of reach, and then left her on her own.

He dropped the phone onto the floor and walked over to her, kneeling in front of her. 'Alex, I'm so sorry.'

'It's okay.' One tear trailed down her cheek and she brushed it away. 'I'm used to thinking about these things. You shouldn't have to.'

That wasn't the way it had been last night. But he'd messed up badly and he couldn't expect her to allow him the precious trust that she'd shown last night. 'I'll get your bag.'

'Yes, thanks. I'll go and have a shower in the other bathroom, if that's okay.' She smiled up at him. 'There are grab rails.'

He wanted to say that she didn't need grab rails—that she could hold onto him. But the truth was that she did— because he couldn't be relied on, couldn't be the man she deserved.

'You've finished your calls?' She nodded at the phone, lying on the floor.

'Oh. Yeah. Nothing urgent.' Another layer of misery folded around his heart. That was the real reason for her tears. He'd got out of bed so hurriedly that he couldn't have failed to wake her up, and she'd heard him downstairs. It felt almost as if he'd been caught being unfaithful to her. Leo was under no illusions that he'd betrayed her trust.

He stood, catching up his jeans from the washing basket and pulling them on. It was suddenly chilling to be this naked in front of her. 'I'll bring your bag, and then I'll go and get us something to eat.'

She nodded. 'Thanks. That would be nice.'

Alex had gulped down the coffee he'd made and pushed the banana pancakes around on her plate, in a gesture towards eating them.

'What are you doing today?' Maybe she'd stay and they could try to work this out. Although Leo couldn't think how they were going to do that.

'I should get home. I…' She shrugged.

'You're not coming back, are you?' He'd seen women decide not to come back before, and he knew the signs. Maybe time had softened the memory, but he didn't recall it hurting quite as much as this.

'No, I need… With my leg, Leo, I need to…' She lapsed suddenly into silence.

'If you want to give me a reason then give one. If you don't, that's fine. But the one thing I won't take from you is that it's because of your leg, Alex. That's not a reason and we both know that.'

'Yes, we do.' She gave a sudden, all too brief, smile. 'I need to feel that you might be able to…that for just some of the time you can forget everything else and be with me, without regretting it afterwards. I don't think that's going to happen.'

He could tell her that it would. He could tell her he'd make it happen, but he'd be lying. The panic he'd felt this morning, the tearing regret that he'd been so stupid as to lose himself with Alex, had been a gut reaction but it had been there. She deserved a great deal more than that.

'No, it's not. I'm sorry, Alex.'

'We took a risk and it didn't work out. That's okay.' She looked up at him suddenly. 'Would you do something for me, please?'

'Of course.'

'I want you to delete my number from your phone. And I'll delete yours. I don't want us to be...' Alex gave a little shrug.

She didn't need to explain. The sudden impulse to beg her not to was almost too much for Leo, but he knew this was the right thing to do. 'You don't want me to be looking at my phone, wondering if you've called, do you. Because you're not going to.'

'No. I'm not.'

It seemed so final, but at least this was real. In some ways this was the most compassionate thing she could have done, in a situation that was tearing him apart. Leo took his phone from his pocket and, with shaking fingers, he found her number and deleted it. When he looked up, he saw that Alex was doing the same.

She stood up, seeming to shed whatever she felt about that, suddenly brisk. 'I should get going.'

He fetched her bag from upstairs, trying not to look at the rumpled bed. Trying not to smell the faint scent of their lovemaking, which still perfumed the air. By the time he got back downstairs, she was in her coat and looking for her car keys in her handbag.

'I'll take your things to the car...'

Alex shook her head. 'I can manage. Thank you.' She took her bag and turned, opening the front door. Leo watched her go. Across the bridge, alone this time. Then she put her things into the car and the engine choked uncertainly into life.

He wanted to shout the words after her, but he could only whisper them. Because shouting them might elicit some response from her, and he knew that he should just let her go.

'Be happy.'

CHAPTER SIXTEEN

HER KNEE STILL throbbed a little from when she'd crashed down on all fours. She'd woken with a start when Leo had got out of bed, and realised almost immediately that she'd lost him. Swinging herself out of bed and across the room should have been easy—she'd managed enough times before—but she'd been so shaken by grief that she'd fallen.

Somehow, she made it down the track without either driving into the millpond or crashing into a tree. But any further and tears would have blinded her. Alex pulled off the road into an entranceway to a field, switched off the engine and then crashed her fist into the steering wheel.

This might feel a little better if she hated Leo. If she could convince herself that he wasn't a good man. If he hadn't made love to her that way last night. He'd meant it. She knew he'd really meant it.

But none of that mattered. Leo had just been on loan to her. For one gorgeous night she'd thought that he could live for the moment, in the here and now, and then the past had clawed him back again. Alex couldn't forget the guilt and regret on his face when he'd appeared in the doorway. Last night had meant something to both of them and that look had taken it all back, soured and destroyed it.

She pulled a tissue from the glove compartment. She was going to cry. She could feel it welling up inside, an insistent and wordless agony. All she could do was to get it over with. She'd fallen down and, however much it hurt, she was going to have to get back up again.

Getting back up again hadn't been so easy. Alex missed Leo every day. Every time she walked past the cake shop on the way to the charity's office. Every time someone wrote to her or phoned her, saying that they'd heard her on the radio.

The dark days of March trickled away and became the slightly less dark days of April. It would be summer soon. Alice had been fitted for her running blade and was beginning to learn to run with it. She'd asked Alex to put a photograph up on the charity's website, in the hope that the anonymous donor might see it and know how much it meant to her. Perhaps Leo would. Perhaps he'd see it and smile.

'Look at these!' Rhona came flying into the office, a bunch of yellow roses in her hand, her face flushed with pleasure.

'They're lovely. You and Tom had a good weekend, then?'

'It was a great weekend. But Tom doesn't send yellow roses—he sends red ones. And not two dozen long-stemmed ones either; we're saving for the wedding.' Rhona put the flowers down on Alex's desk. 'These are for you.'

'Me?' Two dozen long-stems sounded suspiciously like Leo. Or maybe he was just the first person who sprang to mind because she'd been thinking about him again, on her way to work this morning.

'You. Yellow roses. That's for friendship, in case you were wondering.'

'Who are they from?' Alex didn't dare touch them. If they weren't from Leo then it meant they must be from someone else. And receiving roses from someone else felt somehow disloyal. Even if there was nothing between her and Leo any more.

'How do I know?' Rhona rolled her eyes and plucked a small envelope from the side of the wrapping. 'It's knobbly…'

'Well, what is it?'

'Oh, for goodness' sake.' Rhona opened the envelope and took out a thumb drive. 'Here. Roses and electronic media. And…'

She handed the card to Alex. Leo's firm, flowing handwriting.

Thank you.

She dropped the card onto her desk as if it had just burned her fingers.

'So they are from Leo?' Rhona raised her eyebrows.

'Yes.'

Rhona slumped into her chair. 'What do you want to do about it, honey?'

'I… I don't know. I can't do anything about it.' She and Rhona had been through all this. She'd taken a risk and it hadn't worked out. That had hurt so badly that she couldn't take another.

'What do you say I put the flowers in water and go down and get a couple of coffees from the shop? Then we'll think about the thumb drive.'

'Okay. Thanks.' Alex pushed the flowers away from her as if they might burn her.

The flowers were arranged, coffee was fetched, and she and Rhona sat in front of Rhona's computer.

'Sure you want me to see this?' Rhona slotted the thumb drive into the USB port.

'Yeah. It's okay. Yellow roses, right?' The message was friendship. It was probably photographs from the radio station, something like that.

Rhona clicked on a folder and then on the icon inside. A sound file. A familiar jingle sounded through the speakers and the two women looked at each other. It was Leo's medical hour.

'You want me to turn it off…?'

'No. Listen with me.' She'd come this far and she couldn't go back now.

Then Leo's voice. At first, all she could hear was the smooth, sexy sound and then she began to focus on what he was actually saying.

'We've tackled a lot of very difficult issues here on the medical hour, and we pride ourselves on making this a place for people to talk. I've come to understand that sharing our experiences is not just a way of healing for ourselves, but for others, which is why I've decided to talk about this very personal issue. My twin brother took his own life when we were twenty-two. I'm pleased to welcome Dr Celia Greenway, who is a consultant psychologist…'

'He's talking about Joel…' Alex turned to Rhona, her hand over her mouth, tears streaming down her face.

'Who? Never mind. Are we sticking with it?'

'Yes… Yes.'

A woman was talking now…

'Leo, I've spoken at some length with both you and your family, and I want to make it clear to everyone listening that Leo and his family have given me permission to speak about some of the personal issues that came out of our discussions. What would you say was the most difficult emotion for you?'

'Guilt… I wasn't able to talk about some of the things which happened on the night of my brother's death for many years.'

'In fact, not until you and your family talked to me?'

'No…'

He was going to crack up. Alex could hear it in his voice. But somehow, through an obvious effort of will, Leo was holding it together. He spoke to each caller in turn, encouraging them to talk and answering all of the questions that were put to him honestly. With the usual jingles and the break for the news edited out, the recording lasted three-quarters of an hour, and Alex and Rhona listened in silence.

Finally, he wrapped the programme up.

'I want to thank Celia for being with us—with me—tonight and, as I said, the lines will be open for another hour so that anyone who'd like a call-back can leave their number. And finally I want to thank the very special person whose own courage inspired me to take this first step tonight. Goodnight, everyone.'

Rhona let out a long breath. 'That whole programme was *the* most moving thing I've heard in a long while.'

'Yes.' Alex felt almost numb.

'What does it mean?'

'It means…' She shrugged. 'He means exactly what he says. Leo always means what he says on the radio.'

'He wants…you and him?'

'No. It's what he said. He's taking the first step on a long road. It takes a long while to turn a life around.'

'So what are you going to do?'

'I don't know.' Alex thought hard. 'Yes, I do. Those pictures of Alice you took the other day, with her blade…'

'Alice?' Light dawned suddenly on Rhona's face. '*He* was the anonymous donor?'

Alex nodded.

'That's generous.' Rhona nodded in approval. 'You know, I thought he was a bit of a rotter at first, but he's not such a bad guy at all.'

'No. He's a very good guy. Just not *my* guy.'

If anything, Leo's message had given Alex some closure, and she guessed that maybe that had been his intention. She was getting back on her feet again. Bruised and still feeling broken, but she was getting there.

Justin's voice on the phone didn't make her heart leap, hoping that he had some news of Leo. She knew what Leo was doing, and he wished her well, and she could put those thoughts away now.

'Alex, how are you?' Justin didn't stop for an answer. 'I want to ask you a favour.'

'What is it?' As long as it had nothing to do with Leo, she'd be happy to do whatever Justin asked.

'Will you listen in at ten tonight? Just for fifteen minutes.'

'Ten o'clock? That's the music hour, isn't it?'

'Yes, on Friday nights it's two hours. But that doesn't matter. All I'm asking is fifteen minutes. I need you to promise.'

Whatever this was, Justin was being a bit overdramatic. But that was Justin. 'Okay. Fifteen minutes, at ten o'clock. What do you want me to do then?'

'Feedback. That's all. Do you promise?'

'Yes, I promise.'

'Fantastic. I'll put you on the list. Got to go…'

Alex settled down on the sofa with a cup of tea and a pencil and pad, and switched on the radio at exactly ten o' clock. She'd listen for fifteen minutes, give her feedback and then go to bed. There was going to be a climbing group going down to Sussex tomorrow and she had to be up early.

'And this is Clemmie Rose, with two hours of music for you to keep you cool and relaxed on a Friday evening. If there's someone out there you want to send a message to, then just call in. But first…'

Alex picked up her pencil. This must be it.

'Hi, Clemmie.'

What? When Leo's voice sounded on the radio Alex threw her pencil back down in disgust. What was Justin playing at?

'You want to say something, I gather?'

'Yes. This is a message for Lieutenant Tara—'

'*The* Lieutenant Tara?' Clemmie interjected.

'No, not *the* Lieutenant Tara. *Me*. He means me,' Alex shouted crossly at the radio.

'The lady in question knows who I mean, and this is my message to her.'

'Go ahead, Leo.'

'Well, stop interrupting him then…' Alex had really liked Clemmie when she'd met her. Now she was beginning to get on her nerves.

Leo spoke, his voice clear and impassioned. 'There's no reason on earth why you should even listen, but I'm begging you to think about what I have to say. I love you and I want you to take me back. I promise I won't let you down this time.'

'What? Leo, you can't be serious…' Could he? He sounded serious.

Clemmie's voice again. 'Well, I can tell you that this guy surely looks as if he means it. So if the lady in question has an answer and would like to phone in we'll put her straight through. And, in the meantime, as it's you, Leo, I'm going to let you choose the next track.'

'Thanks. It's a song from Bobby and Aleesha's new album.'

'Ooh—*love* that. It's a new direction for both of these two, but it's been selling like hot cakes.'

'Yep. They took a risk, but it worked out. Here's Bobby and Aleesha.'

'No, Leo…' Tears started to roll down Alex's face. How could he do this?

She knew exactly how he could do it. She'd asked him to take her number out of his phone, and she'd taken his out of hers because she wanted no part of Leo's guilt. When he spoke to her, she wanted it to be real. And for Leo, saying it on the radio was about as real as it got.

She got to her feet, her heart thumping and her lungs straining to breathe. He loved her. He wouldn't let her down. Leo had promised.

'Okay. Take a breath. Count to ten.' That didn't work. She started to pace up and down, listening to the radio, wondering whether Leo would come back on.

It seemed not. The song had finished and there were more messages. From Darren to Claire. From Emma to Pete. Her head was spinning, and she still didn't know what to do. Dared she trust Leo?

'And we have Marion from Hampstead on the line. Marion, who's your message for?'

'My message is for Leo. I hope the lady says yes, but if she doesn't then just pass my number on. *I'll* say yes, Leo.'

'No, you won't!' Alex yelled at the radio, picking it up and shaking it hard.

Then she knew. Alex grabbed her phone, staring at it.

She didn't have his number. And, despite the fact she'd heard it about a million times, she couldn't remember the number of the radio station. She waited impatiently for the next piece of music to finish, and then Clemmie obligingly read it out.

She dialled and waited. She knew that if she hung on the call would be answered, but it might take a while. Then she heard the operator on the other end.

'Hello… Hello, it's Alex Jackson…'

'Alex. I have a question for you. What colour was that gorgeous dress of yours?'

'My what?' Suddenly she realised. They were making sure that it was her. 'Green. It was green.'

'Right. Hold on for just one moment. Don't go away—I'm putting you through to Leo.'

A couple of clicks on the line, and then Leo's voice. 'Alex?'

She closed her eyes, wishing that she could see him. 'Leo… Leo, are we on the radio?'

'No. It's just you and me.' Alex jumped as her doorbell rang. 'Is that your bell?'

'Yes, forget it. They'll go away. Leo…'

'I don't think so.' The bell rang a second time.

'Is that you?'

'Yes. I was hoping you might let me in…'

Alex ran to the intercom, slamming her hand onto the door release.

He was coming up. She tugged at the long cardigan she was wearing, pulling it straight, and looked in the hall mirror, pulling her hair out of its ponytail and shaking her head so that it fell around her shoulders. Then her panic subsided. Leo loved her. He'd always taken her just the way she was.

There was a quiet rap on the door and she flung it open. Leo.

He looked amazing. Dinner jacket, bow tie, white shirt. Beautiful, beautiful blue eyes.

'Leo…' She hardly dared breathe. Didn't dare touch him in case this was a dream and he'd suddenly evaporate.

'May I come in?'

She stepped back from the door and he walked into the hallway. 'You heard what I said on the radio? Can you believe me?'

'Yes. You always tell the truth on the radio.'

'I hoped you'd know that.' He seemed suddenly nervous, that easy charm stripped away from him. 'Will you hear me out, Alexandra?'

She swallowed hard. He'd unnecessarily and quite deliciously taken the time to use all four syllables of her name. 'Always.'

'I've done a lot of thinking, and a lot of talking. I'm letting go of the past and that's allowed me to take hold of the present.'

'Live for the moment?'

'I'm living for this moment, right now.'

She could feel it, see it in his eyes. The way she had when they'd made love.

'What you did…that hour on the radio, talking about Joel. It was amazing, Leo. It must have been so hard for you.'

'It wasn't as hard as losing you.' He reached out, taking her hand. 'I love you, and I know we can make this work. Will you take me back?'

Her heart thumped in her chest. But everything was suddenly crystal-clear. Alex cradled his hand between hers, raising it to her lips. 'I should never have left you, Leo. I should have believed in you—you always believed in me, and you took me just the way I am…'

'You *did* believe in me. You never could accept the way I used to be because you knew I could be a better man. That's how I came to believe it too.'

'I love you, Leo. I won't ever let you go again, I promise.'

He let out a sigh, as if finally he could start breathing again. They both could. 'Forever is a long time.'

'We're going to need it. We have a lot to do together.'

Suddenly he grinned. Leo fell to one knee in front of her, taking the red rose from his lapel and putting it into her hands. 'I love you, Alex. And I won't let you down.'

'What are you doing? Leo…' She felt suddenly breathless with joy.

'You know what I'm doing.'

'But… I'm such a mess. And you look so wonderful.'

'You're the most beautiful woman I've ever seen. I'm just overdressed.' He tugged at his bow tie, leaving it to drape around his neck, and pulled open the top two buttons of his shirt. 'Better?'

'Yes. Much better.' They could make this happen. Together they could do it.

'Will you marry me, Alexandra?'

She knew the answer to that too. One word that promised everything. 'Yes.' She reached forward to pull him to his feet. 'I love you so much, Leo, and I really want to marry you. Please, kiss me…'

But Leo had something else on his mind. Reaching into

his pocket, he drew out a ring. A solitaire diamond, which flashed in the light. Alex gasped, covering her mouth with one hand.

'Leo, that's beautiful. It's too much.'

He grinned. 'I could take it back and get a smaller one, if that's what you want.'

'Don't you dare.'

He laughed, slipping the ring on her finger, and then he did the one thing she'd been wanting him to do. The only thing that could make her completely happy. He got to his feet and kissed her.

EPILOGUE

Two years later...

LEO WAS NO longer able to exactly pin down the happiest day of his life. When Alex had told him she would marry him, he'd thought that had to be it. Until the day she *did* marry him. And then the night they'd spent at the secluded beach house on their honeymoon.

As he'd learned to build a life that wasn't bound by guilt he *had* stumbled along the way, but Alex had always been there, stopping him from falling. Helping him find his feet, and love her a little more each time. And he'd been there for her too, encouraging her to take the step of working full-time for Together Our Way and to extend its services. The night she'd collected a Charity of the Year award, he'd thought his heart would burst with pride.

When she'd whispered in his ear that she was going to have his child, Leo had thought nothing could ever make him happier. Then came the moment that he held his new-born daughter in his arms, counting her fingers and toes, and promising little Chloe that he'd always be there for her.

There were the little things too. When Alex told him that she loved him. When she reached for him in the night, and when he caught her up from their bed to watch the sun rise. When he looked into her eyes and saw joy.

It was a summer's morning and Chloe, ten months old now, had slept in the car all the way down to the house in Surrey. He parked the car and Alex walked on ahead with Chloe, her dress flapping in the warm breeze, and stopped at the middle of the bridge to wait for him. As he walked towards them in the sunshine, Chloe stretched out her arms towards him.

'Daddee…'

Alex caught her breath. 'That's right, sweetheart. That's Daddy. Say it again.' She hugged their daughter and Leo dropped the bags he was carrying, hurrying towards them.

'Daddy.'

Alex laughed with delight and he caught the two of them in his arms, hugging them tight. 'Have you been teaching her to say that while my back's turned?'

'No. It's the first time. I've been trying to get her to say, *Daddy, can I borrow the car keys?* But I don't think she's up to that yet.'

'I'm working on, *Mummy, let's go and make Daddy breakfast in bed.* She nearly managed it the other day.'

'I can think of much better things to do with you in bed than feed you breakfast.'

Leo laughed. 'Are you being nice?'

Alex brushed a kiss against his lips. 'I'm never nice.'

If he hadn't known better, and that there would always be more, Leo would have said that *this* was the happiest day of his life.

* * * * *

MILLS & BOON®

MEDICAL ROMANCE™

THE ULTIMATE IN ROMANTIC MEDICAL DRAMA

A sneak peek at next month's titles...

In stores from 26th January 2017:

- **A Forever Family for the Army Doc** – Meredith Webber
- **The Nurse and the Single Dad** – Dianne Drake

0117/03.2

MILLS & BOON®

EXCLUSIVE EXTRACT

Kate Ashton's night with Sam Ryder leads
to an unexpected consequence—but can he
convince this nurse that their love is meant-to-be?

Read on for a sneak preview of
THEIR MEANT-TO-BE BABY
by Caroline Anderson

'You didn't tell me you were a nurse,' Sam said.

'You didn't tell me you were a doctor.'

'At least I didn't lie.'

Kate felt colour tease her cheeks. 'Only by omission.
That's no better.'

'There are degrees. And I didn't deny that I know
you.'

'I didn't think our...'

'Fling? Liaison? One-night stand? Random—'

'Our private life was anyone else's business. And
anyway, you don't know me. Only in the biblical sense.'

Something flickered in those flat, ice-blue eyes, something wild and untamed and a little scary. And then Sam
looked away.

'Apparently so.'

She sucked in a breath and straightened her shoulders.
At some point she'd have to tell him she was pregnant,
but not here, not now, not like this, and if they were
going to have this baby, at some point they would need
to get to know each other. But, again, not now. Now

Kate had a job to do, and she was going to have to put her feelings on the back burner and resist the urge to run away.

Don't Miss
THEIR MEANT-TO-BE BABY
By Caroline Anderson

Available February 2017
www.millsandboon.co.uk

Give a 12 month subscription to a friend today!

Call Customer Services
0844 844 1358*

or visit
millsandboon.co.uk/subscriptions

G